Tales of the Were

Rocky

Bianca D'Arc

ROM
D'Arc

This book is a work of fiction. The names, characters, places, and incidents are products of the writer's imagination or have been used fictitiously and are not to be construed as real. Any resemblance to persons, living or dead, actual events, locale or organizations is entirely coincidental.

Cover Art by Tibbs Design

First electronic publication: December 2012
First print publication: March 2013

ISBN: 1482706725
ISBN-13: 978-1482706727

DEDICATION

This book is for the fans and readers who have helped me through so many difficulties with their uplifting words and kind thoughts. You are a treasure!

I'd also like to give a shout out to the Wild West Wednesday crew for providing fun, friendship and good times that have been sorely lacking in my life over the past three years. With particular regards to Kim Rocha and the Book Obsessed Chicks, the Scarangella family who are each unique and utterly kind hearted, and the writers that make up International Heat, for welcoming me and being like a big, semi-dysfunctional family of mostly like-minded insane writers. I love you guys! Special thanks to my friend Michele Lang for the encouraging write-ins and pep talks. I'm blessed to have all of you in my life.

And I'm especially blessed to still have my father in my life. Thanks, Dad, for your support and understanding, even though you will never read any of my romance stories.

And to Mom, whom I miss every single day. Thanks for watching over us down here and for being the teacher and guide I needed when I was young. I still hear your words, even though I will never hear your voice or cute accent again. *Ik houd van jou.*

PRAISE FOR BIANCA D'ARC'S WRITING

"A truly fantastic read! With a page-turning plot, dynamic characters and plenty of heat, readers will devour every last delicious page." – 4.5 Stars and TOP PICK from *RT Book Reviews Magazine* for **Wolf Hills**.

"No one does dragons like Bianca D'Arc...she continues to awe with her characters and her fertile imagination." – 5 Angels and Recommended Read from *Fallen Angel Reviews* for **The Ice Dragon**.

"...a fantastic read. Ms. D'Arc creates characters that inspire dreams of love and romance in the most jaded reader. Her world building skills are absolutely the best...Anyone who likes dragons and magic should scoop up this book and read it as soon as possible." – 5 Cups from *Coffee Time Romance Reviews* for **Prince of Spies**.

"Bianca D'Arc hits yet another home run... With incredible detail and a wealth of emotion, Ms. D'Arc weaves a tale of redemption that is deep and tremendously poignant." – 5 Blue Ribbons from *Romance Junkies* for **FireDrake**.

CHAPTER ONE

All Hallows Eve

Maggie pulled into the gravel driveway, uncertain of her welcome. The sad truth was she had nowhere else to turn. The pains were getting sharper and closer together. She had to find him soon. After a few false leads, this had to be his place. It just had to be.

She took a deep breath, pulling the car to a stop in front of a very large, rustic log cabin in the middle of the woods. Resting her forehead against the steering wheel as she was wracked by another pain, she tried not to scream.

"Are you all right?"

The deep voice was just as she remembered it. Finally, she had found him. Turning to look out the open driver's side window, she offered him a shaky smile as the pain began to subside.

"Thank heaven I found you. God, Rocky. It's good to see you."

Rocco Garibaldi was stunned. The last person he'd expected to see pull up in his front drive was Maggie Hobson. She was as beautiful as ever, even with deep circles under her gorgeous eyes. She'd gained a bit of weight too, if he wasn't mistaken, and it looked good on her.

"Maggie? What in the world —"

He broke off as her knuckles tightened on the steering wheel and a keening cry ripped from between her compressed lips. In a flash, he had her car door open and then stopped, struck speechless by her rounded, pulsating midsection. Maggie was heavily pregnant, and from all appearances was in the throes of labor.

"I need your help," she panted between puffing breaths.

"No kidding." He caught her when she tried to get out of the tall SUV on her own. Lifting her in his arms, he wasted no time. He took her into his house, went directly to his bedroom and placed her on the bed. "Stars, Maggie! Where's Tony? Why aren't you with him for this?"

"Tony's..." Her beautiful eyes filled with pain and she seemed unable to speak the next, final words. "He's dead, Rock."

Agony settled in Rocky's chest as he felt the truth of her words echo through his soul. His grief was reflected in her sad eyes. He'd lost a brother and he hadn't even known it.

"When? How?"

"About eight months ago. He saw it coming. He had time to warn me about—" A new labor pain struck and Rocky reached for her hand, letting her hold on to him. He hated seeing her in such agony.

"You need help," he said as the pain eased. "Let me call Allie."

Maggie started to get up as he turned toward the phone on the small table beside the bed.

"I knew I shouldn't have come, but Tony made me promise to find you before I gave birth. I have nowhere else to turn."

Rocky soothed her, pushing her back down on the bed as he snagged the cord of the phone and pulled it toward him. "You're not going anywhere until that baby is born."

"Babies. Plural." She panted. "Twins."

"Sweet Mother in Heaven," he whispered. "Maggie, did Tony tell you about us? About what we are?"

She nodded once, her expression tinged with fear. "The week before he died, he showed me..." She gripped his hand as another contraction hit. "He warned me the birth wouldn't be easy, and that I couldn't go to a regular hospital. Damn, I'd give anything for an epidural right now!"

Rocky dialed the phone with one hand while she clenched the other tightly. He was never more relieved than when the call was answered on the other end.

"Rafe, I need help."

Maggie loved the rumble of Rocky's voice. It

reassured her in so many ways. Many girlhood hours had been spent dreaming about this man. She found it strange that fate would send her to his home in the middle of the woods, so many years later, about to give birth to his best friend's babies.

Make that cubs. She was about to birth grizzly shifters. If not for the fact she'd seen Tony shapeshift right before her eyes, she would never have believed it. Rocky ended the call as she watched him.

"Tony said..." She waited to catch her breath, needing something to focus on other than the pain. "He said...you're a grizzly too."

Rocky nodded solemnly. "I am."

"This is all so crazy." She looked away, remembering. "Tony came home one day and told me. I almost laughed in his face—until he shifted to prove his point. I was never so frightened in my whole life." She turned back to search his expression. "He only told me because he foresaw his own death, Rock. Something called *Venifucus* was on his trail, he said, and made me promise to tell you as soon as I found you."

"*Venifucus*? Are you certain?" His words were a low growl that sent shivers down her spine.

"He was sure of it, and told me how to retrieve this after he was gone." She tugged on the gold chain around her neck, pulling it out from under her clothing and showing it to Rocky. The pendant was a faintly glowing blood red stone wrapped in gold wire. It was a bear totem that shone brighter than any gem. With shaking hands, she held it up so Rocky could see it.

His expression hardened and a single tear trailed

4

down his face.

"He really is dead."

She nodded, feeling his pain as her own. "I burned his body after he died, as he instructed, then sifted through the ashes for this. He called it—"

"A heartstone." Rocky's expression was filled with an odd mix of wonder and sorrow. "If anyone could do it, Tony would have that kind of magic. But why? How did he die?"

Another contraction halted her explanation for a few moments, and he held her hand throughout. The pulsing heartstone seemed to comfort her, as it had all along her ragtag journey over half the continent.

"He was ambushed. He barely made it home before collapsing. He was beyond help by that point. It only took him moments to breathe his last, but he did it on his home territory, free and safe. He told me the magical protections he'd put on our land would fade after he died, but I would have time to fulfill his last wishes. I followed his instructions and lit out of there just hours later. I've been crisscrossing the country ever since, but I knew when my labor started, I'd have to stop running. I came to you, like I promised Tony I would. My babies will be too vulnerable while I'm recovering—if I survive their birth—and you're the only person on earth I trust to keep them safe." She clutched at his hand. "I don't care what happens to me. Just promise you'll take care of my babies."

Rocky surprised her by taking her in his arms and burying his face in her hair as she burrowed into his neck. It felt so good to be surrounded by his warmth, his strength. It had been so long since she'd been able to lean on someone, even for just a moment.

"I'll keep you safe. You're not going anywhere, Maggie. I'll watch over you all. I promise. Tony knew I would. It's why he sent you to me. But why did you wait so long? You should've come to me straight away."

"I couldn't." Tears leaked from her eyes and seeped into his flannel shirt. He was so strong and she'd felt so weak for so long. It was such a relief to have someone to share her fears with. "I didn't want to lead them to you. I'd just lost Tony and we hadn't heard from you in a long time. I didn't want to presume..."

"You should have, sweetheart. You had to know I'd never turn you away in a million years."

She sniffled as he pulled back to place a kiss on the crown of her head. The gesture touched her deeply—so deeply—when she hadn't dared hope he would welcome her. She'd spent the last eight months conflicted. She'd lost her husband, which was traumatic enough, but Tony had known how she'd always felt about Rocky. Tony had been a shaman. He'd known things, and he'd sent her straight to the only man who had ever been a rival for her affections.

But Rocky had left so long ago. Right after the wedding, he had announced his move and she hadn't seen him since. For all she knew, he was married with children of his own now, though judging by the sparseness of his house, he lived alone. The thought brought a lightness to her heart. Perhaps it wasn't too late for them. Perhaps Tony had been right to send her here. Perhaps she *did* have that chance for happiness again—as Tony had promised—once this situation with the *Venifucus* was straightened out. If it could be straightened out.

Another pain gripped her and she clung to Rocky, digging her fingers into his thick muscles, but he didn't complain. He just held her, speaking soothing words in that rumbly voice and stroking her back with one hand while his other hand moved down to cover the protrusion of her stomach. His touch felt good. When his fingers settled over the beach ball of her abdomen, it was as if the squirming babies within sensed his presence and immediately quieted.

Tony had warned her how difficult it could be for bear shifter cubs to be born. She was scared and she knew her fear was communicating itself to her babies. As she grew more agitated, so did they. It had been like that throughout her entire pregnancy. She tried to be calm, but the pains were intense and more than she could handle alone. Rocky's steady presence was a gift. He calmed her and her babies with just his touch, his voice and his soothing strength.

She didn't fear much of anything with Rocky's arms around her. He was her safe harbor in times of trouble and had been since they were kids. When bullies picked on her in grade school, it had been Rocky who had come to her rescue and scared off the other kids with his intimidating brawn, even back then. He'd been such a quiet boy, but she'd daydreamed about him from that moment on. He had been her knight in shining armor, her champion and savior.

Tony, on the other hand, had been her Prince Charming. They'd all grown up together, and by the time the senior prom rolled around, Maggie had despaired of Rocky ever seeing her as a girl instead of a buddy. But Tony had. He'd asked her to the prom and suddenly her eyes had been opened. Here was a man who flattered her and charmed her. Tony had literally swept her off her feet. After that first date, he'd sought her out again and again. Before she knew it, she was head over heels in love with him and agreeing to his proposal of marriage.

The only doubts had crept in when they'd broken the news to Rocky. He'd looked pained for one short moment before offering his congratulations. Still, she was in the bloom of young love and very little could dim the light that shone around Tony. He was such a charismatic, powerful presence in her life. She was grateful for his love, even now, after all the turmoil being with him had caused.

Still, she was glad Tony had acknowledged Rocky once more before he died. Tony had given her careful instructions. He wanted her to go to Rocky. And after eight months of running, she finally had.

CHAPTER TWO

Rocky moved back, sensing others outside the cabin. "Are you okay? I've got to let them in."

"Who?" Panic filled her eyes as she clutched at his arms.

He soothed her, stroking her back. "Friends. Guardians. They'll help us, but they need to know what they're up against."

She grabbed his hands when he would have stood, her eyes frightened. "Tony said the man chasing me is a very strong mage. He almost caught me a few times, but the babies warned me."

So they were already aware and strong magically, but then their father had been one of the most powerful bear shifter shamans in recent memory. No doubt they'd inherited some of their father's talents.

"We've faced *Venifucus* before. As long as we know what to look for, we can protect you. You did the right thing coming here, but you should've come much sooner, Maggie." He stood and moved to the door.

He had to get out of the cabin for just a minute. Emotions stirred in his heart that he hadn't felt in years. Seeing Maggie again was bringing up all the old feelings and conflicts, but one thing was very different this time. This time, Tony would not present an obstacle.

Tony was gone.

The reality of it hit him as he walked through the door into the discordant sunshine, his steps faltering. He reached out to steady himself on the doorframe when a strong hand wrapped around his arm. He recognized the energy. Tim.

"What is it, Rock?"

Rocky tried to shake off the pang of grief, but knew the Alpha wolf could sense his deep sorrow. Rocky met Tim's eyes. "My brother is dead."

Tim did a very uncharacteristic thing. He pulled Rocky into hug right there on the doorstep, and Rocky went, glad of the unquestioning support of his friend and leader.

"The woman you mentioned?" Tim asked as he pulled back. "His wife?"

Rocky nodded, getting a grip on the turmoil in his soul. "She's human, Tim. She needs help. Bear cubs don't come easy."

Tim nodded. "Allie and Betina are on their way with Rafe. They were in town and he went to fetch them. I've got some of the Pack coming to set up a perimeter. No one will get to her."

"She's being chased by *Venifucus*. A strong mage, she said. And he'd have to be very powerful to take down Tony. He was a gifted shaman, Tim. No simple mage could match Tony."

Tim placed one hand on his shoulder, offering reassurance. "We have allies, my friend. We'll call on them all, if need be."

Rocky cleared his throat. "Thank you, Alpha."

Just then a feminine gasp of pain sounded from inside the bedroom that was in the front of the house, just a few feet away. Rocky turned to look through the bedroom door, only to see Maggie's abdomen rippling in an alarming way. He went to her side in a blur of movement. Instinctively, he called on his inner magic, covering the protrusion of her belly with his hands and concentrating his power on soothing the babies inside. They calmed and the agony on Maggie's face lessened.

"Please! Don't leave me again, Rocky."

He met her gaze. "Never."

A moment passed, and the contraction eased. Rocky sat on the bedside, glad he'd opted for a king size even though he usually slept alone. He stroked her abdomen with one hand, trying to ease her into a more comfortable position with the other.

"The priestesses are on their way, and the Alphas are gathering the Pack to guard us. You're safe now, Maggie. I promise." His words seemed to soothe her, so he kept talking as he touched her, enjoying the sensation.

She was so soft and feminine. She was all he'd ever wanted in a woman. He'd never touched her so freely in his life, but she needed him now. She needed the reassurance of his touch—anyone's touch—he guessed. She needed to know she wasn't alone. She needed to feel safe so her cubs would come into the world as peacefully as possible.

"Priestesses?" she repeated, sounding a little dazed. "Rocky, I'm Catholic."

That startled a laugh out of him and brought an answering smile to her face, though she still looked a little worried. "Shifters are closer to nature than humanity. We have always served the Lady in Her many forms. Call Her Mother Nature if it helps, though she's been represented in many different religions, including yours. The women who are coming to help you are Her servants. They have a great deal of magic and skill between them. It'll help you and your babies, Maggie. Your babies are part of Tony. They're magic. They need magic to help them be born."

"You're magic too." She surprised him by covering his hand still resting on her abdomen. "They need you too." She paused, looking down at their joined hands. "*I* need you."

Rocky couldn't help himself. He leaned forward and placed a kiss on her forehead, rising only to kiss her swelling tummy, where the little ones kicked and squirmed. They quieted as he stroked their resting place, as if responding to his touch. They seemed to recognize him and he knew in that moment, these babies would be his family. He'd raise them in Tony's stead and be father to them in place of the best friend he'd ever had. These cubs were his now.

As was their mother. Only she didn't know it yet.

Another pain wracked her small body and Rocky's heart twisted. He called on the magic that was his to command—so much less than Tony's had been—and sent it to her and the children, hoping to ease their way. How he wished Tony could be here. Tony was the one with all the magic. Rocky was only good with his fists, and for lifting heavy objects.

Rocco Garibaldi and Antonio Fernandez had grown up together on the outskirts of Whitefish, Montana, brothers in every way but blood. Bear shifters were rare, so when two grizzly families settled in the same area with cubs the same age, they'd sniffed each other out and forged an alliance. As a result, Rocky and Tony had been nearly inseparable from their earliest years.

Tony had been gifted with more than the ample magic already granted to bear shifters, and Rocky had physical strength beyond that of any normal shifter. Rocky was already stronger than most bear shifters when he was still just a teen, and as he grew into adulthood, his size and speed only increased, but Tony was never jealous. Tony was a shaman, and from a young age he could foresee certain things that would come to pass. There was only one point of contention between the two young men as they entered adulthood.

Maggie.

Margaret Hobson was a beautiful girl, and they both loved her, but not even she knew about their ability to turn into grizzlies whenever the mood struck. Their shifting ability was kept a strict secret from their human friends.

Rocky had never been eloquent. He often let Tony do the talking for them both. Tony was brilliant, and while Rocky was no slouch in school—he'd become an engineer, after all—when compared to Tony, he always found himself lacking. He didn't begrudge Tony his native intellectual abilities, just as Tony didn't begrudge Rocky's physical prowess.

Only that one time had Rocky wished he'd had Tony's way with words...and women. That day when he'd lacked the nerve—and the words—to ask Maggie to the senior prom. She'd gone with Tony instead, and from that point on, they'd been a couple. Just a few years later, they'd married and Rocky had left Whitefish for good.

"Something's happening."

Maggie's shocked whisper brought Rocky back to the moment. The babies were moving, both heading south toward the exit of their temporary home. He could feel it under his palm.

"Whoa there, little ones," he whispered, hoping some sense of his words would make it through to the cubs struggling under his hands. And maybe it did. He could feel them cease their struggles momentarily as if listening. "Maggie, I don't think they want to wait for the priestesses. I think we're going to have to do this ourselves."

Rocky spared her a glance, taking in her terrified, yet trusting expression. The look on her face gave him pause, but the babies demanded his attention. He could feel their plaintive questioning now. They were turning to him for direction, sensing his power, his dominance over them. These amazingly powerful bear cubs recognized their Alpha and awaited instruction.

But they wouldn't wait for long.

"God, Rocky!" She gasped. "I can feel them. They want out."

"I know, sweetheart." He moved around her on

the wide bed, positioning himself to aid her as best he could. Just then he heard a truck roar into his yard, spraying gravel against the wooden siding of the house. He smiled at her, keeping his tentative hold on the babies as he heard the soft tripping of feminine footsteps come up to his door. "They're here. Praise the Lady."

He stood, but Maggie's hand clamped down on his wrist. "Don't leave me!"

Rocky scooted around to the head of the bed, sat beside her and kept his hand firmly over the squirming babies in her tummy. "I'm not going anywhere, Maggie. Never again."

He lifted her slightly so she rested against his arm. She felt so right there. He reached down and kissed her hair, tenderness overwhelming him.

A knock sounded on the door and he cursed the ladies' politeness. Still, he knew it wasn't polite to enter a grizzly's den without permission, even in an emergency such as this.

"Come in." Rocky raised his voice, careful not to blast Maggie in the ear as she leaned against him.

The door opened and a moment later two women bustled in and took over. Betina was a tiny thing, ageless in a fey way and deceptively powerful. Her apprentice, Allie, was younger, earthier, but just as lovely. Both were strong magic users and gentle women he respected greatly. He kept the introductions short, feeling the urgency under his hand. The cubs would wait no longer.

Betina placed her hand over Maggie's, which still rested over Rocky's on her protruding stomach. Rocky would have moved away, but the priestess stopped him.

"We need you to anchor them as their Alpha. Guide them with your knowledge of their true nature." Betina knelt on the other side of the big bed, barely disturbing the mattress.

She smiled serenely at Maggie and Rocky felt the magic in the air, putting Maggie and the cubs more at ease. He knew then he was in the presence of immense power not entirely of this world.

Of course, he'd always had his suspicions about the high priestess. She had a timeless, ageless beauty. It had come clear during their last battle with a *Venifucus* mage that she was not completely human. Only the Lords and their lady knew for certain, but Rocky suspected Betina was more than a little bit fey. It would explain her enormous magic and slender, almost fragile appearance.

Rocky knew the moment Betina spotted the softly pulsing heartstone. Her gaze slid from the necklace upward to meet Rocky's eyes.

"I can feel their sire's magic flowing through these youngsters. They will be very powerful when they are grown."

"Their father was the most gifted grizzly shaman of our generation." Rocky confirmed with a nod.

Betina gave him a kind smile and returned the little nod. "All will be well," she intoned with confidence that communicated itself through her words to all who heard them.

In due course, with Betina's expert guidance and not a little support from Allie and Rocky as well, the babies came squirming into the world, full of magic and the wonder of life. Rocky was almost overwhelmed by the event. He'd never been present at a birth before, and never one accompanied by such positive omens.

It was Samhain after all, what the human world called Halloween. This was a special time for all magical folk. Up until the moment he'd found Maggie sitting in her car in front of his house that afternoon, Rocky had planned to run with the other shifters that night, in celebration of this sacred time. Even now, werecreatures of all kinds were probably gathering in the circle of stones where the ceremony to mark the sabbat would be held.

Samhain was an auspicious time for such a significant birth. Twins were rare. Twin boys of Alpha shaman lineage even more so. It was more than likely that these cubs would be the next Lords when they came of age. Rocky knew no grizzly shifter had ruled the *were* in recent memory. He feared it was a powerful portent of troubling times to come.

CHAPTER THREE

Maggie was tired but in surprisingly little pain. The beautiful apparition who'd come to help her was so gentle and kind, Maggie felt instantly calm in her presence.

"The babies have given you their first gift, Margaret," Betina said as Allie cleaned the infants just a few feet away in the small cabin. "They've healed your body as much as possible. You should be good as new in a few days with a little TLC, which I know our Rocky will be happy to provide. In fact, I'll wager you'd be up for a walk to the glen tonight, if you'd agree to let your babies take part in our celebration."

"Do you really think that's wise?" Rocky asked, his warm voice sounding above her head, rumbling against her back. He was her anchor, her rock, as he always had been when they were younger.

"I think it's important, yes." Betina nodded. "If

Margaret is agreeable."

The high priestess placed her hand on Maggie's forehead and a burst of energy fired through her. It was as if the fog had cleared and suddenly things were sharper and more in focus than they had been.

"What did you do to me?" she asked as she sat up a little straighter, Rocky's strong hands helping her. She felt—if not good as new—certainly not as if she'd just suffered through a day of intense labor and pain, not to mention an arduous twin birth.

Betina smiled. "Fuzzed the edges of your pain a bit, just to help you through. It's the best we can do without drugs, but shifter babies are very sensitive to any kind of chemicals, so we had to do this *au natural*, with a touch of magic, of course." Her tinkling laugh enchanted Maggie. There was something very special about this woman.

"That's amazing. Thank you. I don't know what I would have done without you."

Betina patted her hand as she rose from the messy bed and turned to Allie, who was finished cleaning the squirming infants. Betina placed first one baby and then the other in Maggie's outstretched arms. Rocky was there to help, steadying her and supporting the babies with his big hands, and all felt right with the world.

Rocky marveled at the way Maggie bounced back from what had been the most amazingly painful and joyful experience he'd ever witnessed. She'd been in agony, her grip nearly crushing the bones in his hands as she clung to him through the worst of the ordeal. Betina and Allie had worked their magic to make her unaware for the most part, but it had still been a frightening experience.

He'd helped too, in his way. Tony's babies were more self-aware than any newborn shifters he'd ever seen, and they needed his constant reassuring energy, his direction and dominant authority. They would be handfuls as they grew, he could already tell. Rocky looked forward to taking the youngsters in hand and teaching them the ways of the world.

Maggie's recovery was truly amazing. The priestesses helped clean her up as she cuddled the babies, then helped her to a nearby chair so they could strip the bed of its soiled linens. She had one child in each arm, whispering to them as they settled to sleep next to her warm body. It seemed they too were tired from their ordeal.

"They're beautiful," she whispered.

Rocky couldn't agree more. "Just like their mama." His soft words brought her gaze up to his and they shared a moment of communion, of sharing and joy. Rocky bent to place a kiss on her forehead. "You did good, Maggie."

Her smile brightened his world.

The priestesses cleaned up his bed, making it fresh and taking away the laundry, but Rocky was mostly oblivious to the bustle around him. All that mattered in his universe was the woman sitting in front of him and the two little bundles of magical, loving energy now asleep in her arms.

"What's this about a walk? I know by rights I shouldn't feel this good, but I could use a little fresh air."

Betina popped up next to them and smiled.

"Tonight we celebrate the sabbat of Samhain. The most magical night of the year when the veils between worlds are at their weakest. It is the end of the old year and the beginning of the new. The turning point for many beings, including yourself and your babies this year, Margaret."

"I have something you can wear out in the car. It'll be perfect for you." Allie moved toward the door with the bundle of sheets and towels in her arms. "Just let me get it."

"Can I take a shower?" Maggie asked, uncertain. She looked from Betina to Rocky and back, seeking permission, or maybe advice.

"My shower has a bench. I can program it so you can sit and the jets will reach you."

"Program it?" A hint of a smile curled her lips.

Rocky shrugged with an answering grin. "I may live in the woods, but I like my creature comforts."

"I think a shower wouldn't hurt," Betina advised. "As long as you don't overdo it. You're in much better shape than most women after giving birth, thanks to your sons' magic, but you will need a little time to heal completely. Allie and I will watch over the little ones while you cleanse your body and spirit. It's actually a very good idea to start fresh on the sabbat." Betina beamed at her.

"Thank you. I promise not to overdo it. If Rocky can just program his space age shower for me..." She shot him an amused look. "I'll be fine."

Maggie managed to walk into the surprisingly large bathroom with Rocky and Betina's help. Allie had come back inside and was watching over the babies while they slept. Whatever magic had been done to her, Maggie was feeling better with each passing second.

Entering the bathroom, she stopped short in the doorway. It looked like a little piece of heaven on Earth—in a masculine sort of way. Slate tile covered the heated floor and every wall in soothing shades of blue, grey and tan.

The shower itself was gigantic. It had a slate bench running along one side with ledges placed at strategic heights for soap and shampoo. It fit in one corner of the big bathroom, the walls tiled in matching slabs of natural slate placed in a lovely, almost mosaic pattern. Gleaming silver faucets and showerheads stuck out every now and then from the walls and ceiling. The other two sides of the six foot enclosure were made of glass, artfully frosted with a mural of bears in the woods, interwoven with knot work symbols that spoke to her artistic side.

The entire effect made her feel safe and protected. It also made her covetous. She loved this bathroom and wished she could build one exactly like it for herself.

While she'd been admiring the décor, Rocky had stepped up to a control panel cleverly hidden behind a decorative tile. She watched in fascination as he punched buttons, turning the water jets inside the enclosure on and off until he had it arranged to his satisfaction. She stepped closer, watching over his shoulder, noting that he was able to set both the angle and direction of each of the many water nozzles as well as the water temperature and pressure.

"You weren't kidding when you said you had to

program this thing."

Rocky looked at her over his shoulder and grinned. "It's computer controlled and completely customized to my specifications. I spent a lot of time with the manufacturer going over plans to get it just right."

"Wow." She was impressed. Rocky had always liked gadgets and computers when they were growing up. It didn't surprise her that the trait had followed him into adulthood. "This is fantastic. I think I could spend hours relaxing in here."

"Glad you like it." He seemed uncomfortable with her praise, but she could tell he was pleased.

"This is a work of art, Rocky," Betina said quietly, admiring the glass mural. "Protective, healing magic is worked within these designs."

"I know. I consulted with a friend before I made the panels." He looked almost bashful as he answered the older lady.

"Your work?" Betina seemed surprised, making Maggie want to rise to his defense.

"Rocky was always artistic. He used to sculpt and whittle a lot when we were kids. I have the carvings you gave me and Tony over the years packed in my bags." She turned to him, touching his arm.

A moment of silent communication passed between them, but she wasn't sure what it meant. She wanted him to know how much he'd always meant to her, and hoped the fact that she'd saved his gifts — out of all the things she'd had to leave behind — would mean as much to him as it did to her.

Rocky cleared his throat as the moment ended. He moved toward the door to the giant bathroom.

"I'll bring in your bags from the car and park the SUV in the shed where it can't be seen."

"Thanks." He always thought of everything. She would be safe now. She knew it in her heart.

With Betina's help, she got in the shower and was able to control the jets somewhat with the waterproof controls set into the wall near the bench. She was glad of the slate ledge. Her legs were still a little rubbery, but as she washed the sweat and grime from her body, she started to feel much better.

Betina left her, promising to come at once if Maggie needed help, but she was glad of the few moments alone with the just the warm water and the feeling of security — of Rocky's protection, here in his home — wrapping around her. Maggie wept, knowing her life had changed irrevocably. A new chapter was just starting, and though she feared what might come, she also looked forward to it.

The past had to be put away. Not forgotten, but dealt with so she and her babies could move forward.

She wept for the husband she'd loved so much and lost so unfairly. For the babies who would never meet their father. But her tears were balanced by the hope that they would know him through Rocky. She sensed he would teach them all they needed to know about being little bears.

That thought should have jarred her, but it was becoming more and more familiar to her. More right. Her babies would be able to turn into grizzly bears.

Rubbing soap lather over her sore limbs, she took a moment to really study the glass mural encasing her in its nurturing, protective embrace. The scene was just like the woods she had traveled through to get to

Rocky's cabin. Bears were walking along behind and through the dominating trees. She could see one giant adult bear leading three little ones of differing sizes while two others climbed and played in the trees overhead.

Her gaze tracked the mural around the corner of the enclosure, enchanted by the scene. She could see glimpses of the bears at first, but as she studied the patterns through the leaves and branches, they came clearer. The mural almost seemed alive, and the level of artistry impressed her.

Turning to follow the mural to its end, she gasped and dropped the soap. There, just at the edge of the scene behind a tree, if she looked carefully, was the outline of a woman. A human woman.

It almost looked like…her. Was this a depiction of her family? Rocky's idea of what she could've had with Tony, had he lived? Or was it some prophetic vision of the future?

"How is it going? Do you need any help?" Betina knocked on the door, dragging her from her troubling thoughts.

"I'm fine," she called out over the shushing of the water. "Just finishing up."

Maggie rinsed off and felt even stronger than before. The shower had definitely helped. She shut off the jets and left the steamy enclosure.

A big, fluffy towel was hanging on a warming rack nearby. She luxuriated in its softness and warmth. Rocky really knew how to live, she'd grant him that. He'd spared no expense on his inner sanctum from the quality of the towels, to the computer wizardry of the shower, to the artwork and soothing, natural tile. This room was a haven, no doubt about it.

Allie had laid out a robe for her. It looked like some kind of ornate ceremonial robe, made of thick, warm fabric—a blend of soft wool and cotton, if she wasn't mistaken. It had knot work designs woven into the dark fabric that were pleasing to the eye, complex, yet beautiful in their simplicity.

Maggie's body still ached a little, but her energy level was surprisingly high. She didn't want to face up to her own more complicated clothing, so the robe was just the ticket. She put it on and was immediately surrounded by its warmth. It felt good.

When she stepped out of the bathroom, Rocky moved immediately to her side, offering an arm for support. She took it, glad for his steadying presence.

"You're looking better already." Betina smiled at her and ushered her to the freshly cleaned bed.

Rocky's low dresser was next to it, now topped by a large, emptied drawer filled with a wad of blankets. It was clear what they'd done. Someone—Rocky, most likely—had taken out the top drawer and emptied it. He'd put the wide drawer on top of the dresser and filled it, covering all the hard edges with soft blankets.

Her babies were nestled inside the cushy nest, sleeping. She paused in front of it to touch each little face, count each set of fingers and toes again. These were her sons, and they were perfect.

"Will they be safe up here?" There were no rails, except the sides of the drawer, and it was a long way down.

"Newborns don't move around much," Betina

said. "But one of us will be here watching them while you rest. You have time for a short nap and then we'll see about getting you to the ceremony, if you're still up for it."

She turned to Rocky, who stood beside her. "Do you think it'd be all right? I mean, it's cold out and the babies —"

"Are grizzly shifters. The cold isn't as bad for them as it would be for a purely human baby. Besides, it's not really that cold for this time of year. I bet they'll like it." He winked at her and grinned. "And Betina wouldn't ask you to take part in the ceremony if it wasn't important. These babies..." He seemed to be having a hard time articulating his thoughts. "They're special. Bear shifters are rare. Grizzlies even more so. And twin boys are important to all *were*, not just bear shifters."

She thought about his words and realized it all came down to trust. She trusted Rocky with her life. More importantly, she trusted him with the lives of her babies. If he thought it was okay then she'd do it, if she was able.

"All right. I'll try that nap first and then we'll see."

"Perfect." Betina helped her into the clean bed and tucked her under warm covers while Rocky watched over them both from his imposing height. As he turned to look at the babies, the expression on his face was so tender it almost broke her heart. For the first time in a long time, she felt safe. Like she was finally home.

CHAPTER FOUR

When Maggie woke a short while later, she felt a lot better. The progress she'd made in the hours since the twins' birth was remarkable. Night had fallen in earnest and the babies were just waking up as she did.

Betina was there, helping her by lifting each child and bringing them to her one at a time so she could feed them. They stopped fussing after their little bellies were full and promptly fell back asleep.

Maggie ate a light meal Rocky brought in a little while later. He sat with her as she ate, making small talk about the babies and life in general, but they didn't touch on any subject that was too difficult. They didn't talk about the danger she and her children had brought to his door, but she was never unaware of it. This idle time could end in disaster. For nothing short of disaster had been dogging her tracks for months now.

"So do you want to make an appearance at the Samhain ceremony?" Rocky's tone was encouraging as he sat in the chair next to his bed, keeping her company and watching the babies.

"Is it far?" She wanted to go, but she was also very aware of the ordeal she and the boys had just been through. She didn't want to do anything that might be too much for any of them.

"Not far. I can get you there without much fuss."

She agreed to go, trusting his judgment. She shouldn't have been surprised when he scooped her into his strong arms and carried her all the way. The man was strong as an ox...or a grizzly.

Allie and Betina each carried one of the babies, who behaved beautifully for the women as Rocky led them to the sacred grove. Hidden at the top of the hill in the forest behind his cabin was a circle of stones— like a miniature version of Stonehenge. Maggie never would have believed it if she hadn't seen it for herself. The place was beautiful in a woodsy way. It was overgrown with moss and vines that seemed to part to let the people through.

Maggie saw animals of all kinds surrounding them, both within the circle and without. Betina and Allie walked to the very center of the circle where a slab of stone sat like an altar. That gave Maggie pause, but deep in her heart she knew Rocky would never put her or her babies in any kind of danger.

"Do all these people turn into bears?" she whispered to Rocky as he put her down and they walked the last few steps together. Betina and Allie handed the babies back to her and Rocky while they went about some sort of preparations near the altar. Maggie and Rocky stood back, a few feet behind them.

He chuckled at her words, the deep rumble sending warmth through her. "No, Maggie. Only me." He paused to stroke one large finger over the baby's chubby cheek. "And the cubs."

The night was chilly, but inside the circle of stones it was comfortable enough. It seemed as if the energy of the place kept things warm and comfy, while a soft dusting of snow fell to earth outside in the forest. A snow owl hooted and all within and without the circle quieted while Betina began to sing in the loveliest voice Maggie had ever heard. Allie joined in and the thrum of power amplified through the stones so that even Maggie could feel it.

She knew she was surrounded by magic, but she had no fear. For one thing, Rocky was standing firmly by her side. For another, she didn't feel the same fear, the same warning in her bones that she'd felt for the past months whenever the *Venifucus* drew too close. The savage killer who'd been following her was evil. These people, by contrast, had none of that taint.

Betina motioned her to stand in front of the altar-like stone and she moved forward, glad of Rocky's solid presence beside her. The ceremony was beautiful, the song ringing through the stones and echoing back into the circle. Allie stood behind Betina, flanked by two identical men, both handsome as sin and both quite obviously protective of her. She wondered, looking at those twins, if someday her sons would have the same proud bearing, the same quiet strength.

Betina's song stopped and she spoke a few words about the earth, air, water and fire, then a few other things Maggie didn't quite follow. She caught the part about giving thanks to the Lady, just before her babies decided to wake up and claim all her attention. Squirming, they began to fidget and wiggle so much she almost dropped the one she held. Jumping forward, she used the stone slab for support, mortified when the baby climbed right out of her arms and his swaddling to tumble naked onto the stone. She reached for him, but Rocky's gentle grip held her back as he deposited the other twin next to his brother.

She looked up, blushing heatedly to see a beatific smile on Betina's face. When she looked down again, her babies were no longer human. They were two tiny bear cubs, barely able to stand on their own...paws.

She nearly fainted.

Her children had *paws*.

Rocky caught her shoulders, offering her his immense strength. She needed every bit of it at that moment.

Betina was speaking again and the twin men stepped forward. Each reached out one hand to one of her babies—cubs—touching them gently. Almost immediately a hum of energy pulsed through the clearing and bright swirls of rainbow light moved like a benign whirlwind through the circle, spreading out into the woods all around, lighting up the faces of many animals and people. Many more than she would have imagined. The woods were teeming with creatures and people, all of whom had come to celebrate this event, and were now smiling at the spectacle that seemed to originate from the two sets of twins by the stone altar.

When the men stepped back, the rainbows remained, ambient light over the clearing. The babies weren't bears any longer, she was relieved to see. They were back to human form, kicking their little feet in the air as they wiggled near each other.

"We welcome the next generation." Betina captured her attention once more. "The next set of twin Alphas born of one of the most powerful Clans. More special than any in many years, these two will be Grizzly Clan shaman. May they grow straight and strong with the loving guidance of their parents."

Rocky stepped forward, keeping one arm around Maggie's shoulders for support. "I claim these boys in place of their blood father, my Clan brother, who is gone from this realm. As is my Clan right, and as I know Tony would have wanted, I claim these boys as my own."

A cheer went up and questions crowded Maggie's mind, but there was no time to ask them now. She wasn't sure what he meant by those ritualistic words, but they certainly sounded serious to her. She sent Rocky a questioning glance, but he redirected her attention to Betina, who was looking at her expectantly.

"What are their names?"

"Antonio and James," she said quickly, surprised by the question. She'd decided in the first weeks of her pregnancy to name them for their father, using his first and middle names. She felt Rocky squeeze her shoulder in approval as Betina smiled, making swirling patterns in the air over where her babies now rested quietly, almost asleep once more. They'd had an exciting night for newborns.

Of course, they acted like no newborns she'd ever seen, but she guessed that was to be expected with so much magic in their tiny little bodies. They'd healed her to the point she felt able to attend this gathering, and her energy level was higher than it had any right to be after what she'd been through. Then there was the shifting-into-bears thing that alternately frightened and amazed her. It was such a strange idea, even after having nine months to get used to it.

The rest of the ceremony passed quickly, and then Rocky was helping her wrap up the babies in the little warm blankets Allie had brought. She kept James while Rocky cradled Antonio in one large hand. She could already tell them apart, though to others she supposed they were identical in every way. Still, she knew her babies — and they knew her.

Rocky bundled his new family back to his home, intercepting the congratulatory nods from the other shifters they passed along the way. Maggie was so tired she probably didn't even notice the reverent stares following their path or the way the other people and animals made way and guarded their steps. All babies were precious among the weretribes, but these special twin babies especially so. Their magic and the way it had manifested tonight proved to all that these were indeed the Alpha pair that would rule over the next generation.

He couldn't be any prouder had he fathered them himself. Tony had been his Clan brother, but he'd also been his best friend. They were closer than blood brothers, closer than regular Clan brothers, and they both shared a love for the woman now walking quietly at his side. Tony was gone and Rocky had to stand in his place with the babies. He also hoped their mother would find a place for him in her heart—after it had healed from her loss.

Perhaps he'd have a second chance to woo this special woman. No other had ever touched his heart like her, and frankly, he'd given up looking. No other woman was Maggie. No other woman could tame him and make him want to be a better man. Not the way Maggie could.

He'd loved her for a long time, but when she'd chosen Tony, he'd bowed out with as much grace as he could muster. Now, however, all bets were off. Maggie would have to stay with him. Not only was she still in danger, but the babies needed him. She would realize that soon enough. He would protect her and help raise the cubs, and if the Goddess had any mercy at all, he'd win Maggie's heart in the process.

Their progress down the mountain was much slower than their trip up had been. Maggie walked, treading carefully with the baby in her arms, and Rocky was content to watch over them both. Her strength was returning little by little, and he figured it would do her good to expend a little of the magical energy the boys had gifted her with before they reached his home. He had an idea what they'd find when they got there and wanted to give everyone time to do their own kind of magic.

"What's all this?" Maggie stopped short as they entered the clearing in front of his single story house.

There were a few cars and trucks crowding the available space and about a half dozen people milling around. More than a few had boxes or bundles in their arms. They'd even turned on the outdoor lighting, though shifters had excellent night vision. Some thoughtful soul had put on the lights for Maggie, one of the few humans among them.

"This, my dear..." he strolled forward, smiling broadly as she followed, "...is the *were* community coming together."

"*Were?*"

The question in her voice made him wonder just how much Tony had told her.

"I'm *were*. So are the cubs. So are all these people. They're members of the various Packs and Clans that live in this area."

"But I thought you said you and the boys were the only ones who could turn into bears."

"Grizzlies. Yes. We are one of the rarest Clans. Tim and Rafe run a big Pack though, and most of these folks are wolves."

"Wolves?" She stopped in her tracks, her face alarmed. "*Were.* Wolves?" She enunciated each word, clearly stunned as her voice dropped to a whisper. "Werewolves? For real?"

"For real." Rocky smiled as he nudged her into motion again. The wolves knew they were here but for now, they were keeping their distance. He noted a few grins though, as their sharp ears had undoubtedly picked up on the conversation. Little got past *were* hearing.

Tim and Rafe waited for them near the front door. "Thanks for all this," Rocky said, extending the hand that wasn't cradling a baby for a respectful shake from each of the wolf Alphas.

"It's the least we could do," said Tim, turning to Maggie.

Rocky made the introductions but thought it wiser to wait to discuss Rafe and Tim's roles as Lords of the *were*. The topic was a little too complicated for quick explanation, especially since Maggie's sons were so clearly destined to fill the same position eventually.

"I'm pleased to meet you." Maggie smiled at the twin Alphas.

"The honor is ours." Rafe smiled warmly and made way for Rocky to open the front door. It was unlocked, but once again, few would dare enter the grizzly bear's den without an explicit invitation. "We brought over a few things to help you with the twins."

Rocky went in first to be certain of the home's security, with Maggie close behind, followed by Rafe. Tim stayed outside to organize the Pack members and parcels. Rocky settled Maggie and both babies on the wide bed while he helped position a double-sized crib, changing table, rocker and other bits that would help with the newborns as well as a whole heck of a lot of diapers and clothing for the little tykes.

Within just a half hour, his house had been turned from bachelor pad to nursery. Rocky knew the power of the Pack, but this impressed even him. Each person who came in received a smile and a few words of thanks from Maggie, though Rocky could see the lines of fatigue returning to her beautiful face. She'd been through a hell of a lot in a short time, and though the magic had sustained her, her energy was starting to flag.

Rocky sent the last of the Pack members on their way with his thanks, knowing they and their brethren would be prowling the woods around his house until the danger passed. He locked his door for the first time in years and turned back to find Maggie and the boys fast asleep in the middle of his bed. Gently as he could, he moved the babies one at a time to the twin sized, hand-me-down crib where they would be safe. It had been a gift from Tim and Rafe—their own crib from when they were babies.

He then took a moment to relieve Maggie of her shoes and place a blanket over her. She needed rest more than she needed to get out of the ceremonial robe Allie had lent her. He tucked Maggie in and took a pillow and a few blankets to make a place for himself on the floor. He'd slept in worse places, and he'd do all in his power to keep Maggie and the cubs safe. If that meant sleeping on the floor, so be it.

Rocky intended to stay awake for a bit, keeping watch, but fatigue claimed him unexpectedly. He knew magic when he felt it. Benign magic. Comforting magic. On this most sacred of nights, he felt the blessings directed toward him and his new family from the other side of the veil, and for a shining moment as his eyes drifted closed, he saw the ghostly outline of his best friend, the brother of his heart, as Tony smiled down on them all.

CHAPTER FIVE

Maggie woke in the middle of the night when the babies did. They didn't really cry—not loudly—instead, they made sort of mewling sounds, alerting her that they were hungry. She'd fed them soon after they were born, but this time there was no one around to help.

Disoriented in the strange setting, she slipped her legs over the side of the unfamiliar bed, immediately encountering a warm lump on the floor that made her jump.

"It's only me. Don't be alarmed."

Rocky's voice flooded her senses and she immediately felt safer. Then she realized he was on the floor. There could only be one reason. She'd stolen his bed.

"Aw, Rock. I didn't mean to make you sleep down there. You take the bed. I have to feed the babies anyway."

Rocky stood, a hulking form in the dim light. He'd left a small lamp burning, probably so she'd be able to see when the babies inevitably woke her in the middle of the night. That was just the kind of thoughtful, caring thing Rocky would do for her, because she couldn't imagine he'd need a nightlight for his own comfort.

"I can help, if you need."

Her face heated with embarrassment. Feeding the babies was a very intimate act she wouldn't have hesitated to share with Tony, but she'd never known Rocky intimately. Sure, she'd dreamed about him throughout her youth, but after Tony had swept her off her feet, she'd put thoughts of Rocky out of her head for good. Or so she'd thought.

Tony was gone now and she had come to terms with her loss over the past months. She even knew Tony would wholly approve of her taking up with Rocky, if by some chance this giant of a man was interested in her. But she was nervous. Everything was new. She'd known Rocky for years, but this intimacy was totally foreign…and very exciting.

"I think I can manage, but I'll call if I need you." She stood, resolutely ignoring the way muscles rippled in his chest. He still had his jeans on, but his magnificent chest was bare. Rocky was definitely still drool-worthy. Her high school girlfriends had coined that term and it had fit Rocky back when he played football for the hometown team. It was even more *a propos* now. He'd filled out since high school. He was all man now, and all enticing.

She walked past him, trying not to stare at his

massive biceps and the honed muscles of his abdomen. He was a work of art in living flesh, and it was hard not to look as she crossed the small space between the bed and the oversized crib holding both babies.

The rocking chair beside it had been delivered with the other furniture. Those people had certainly thought of everything. Maggie was glad for the chair. She turned it to face the wall for a tiny bit of privacy.

The moment she stood over the crib the babies stopped making their funny little noises, their eyes blinking open and little arms flailing upwards, seeking her. She picked up the nearest twin and set about changing his diaper, then did the same with the other boy.

When they were clean and sweet smelling again, she picked up the most active one and sat with him in the rocker. She pushed aside the collar of the robe she still wore from the night before to allow the baby room to suckle.

The little mewling cries started up louder this time from the other twin. When they suddenly stopped, she looked over her shoulder in alarm, only to find the baby nestled in one of Rocky's big hands as he rocked the child against his powerful chest.

"I'll keep him company until you're ready." The wink he sent her stole her breath. He looked so natural with the baby in his arms, so perfect, like he really was their father. And perhaps now he was.

"What was all that claiming stuff about during the ceremony?" she asked softly, still facing away from him.

"These cubs are werebears. Unlike most *were*,

they shift right from the get go, as you saw last night. Their animal sides are very strong. Bears — grizzlies most of all — need a strong Alpha presence to help them as they grow. Since you're not a shifter, these boys will need a male Alpha to step in and show them the ropes. That task falls to me as closest kin to Tony."

"You'd take on that kind of responsibility for his sake?" She knew he and Tony had been closer than brothers, but Rocky had a life of his own that very obviously didn't include children of any sort. Now he'd essentially agreed to act as a father to two babies not his own. That had to put a cramp in his lifestyle.

"For his sake and for theirs. These cubs are more special than you know. But most of all, I'm doing it for you, Maggie." His rumbly voice sent warm shivers down her spine while his words sparked a long lost hope.

"I'm flattered."

"Just flattered?" he asked, a wry chuckle in his words.

"Well, relieved too." She paused. It was easier to talk like this, in the intimacy of the night when she wasn't facing him. "And maybe a little hopeful."

Rocky surprised her, coming around the side of the rocker. She looked down to realize the baby at her breast was now fast asleep. Rocky shocked her further, picking up that baby in one giant hand and placing him back in the crib before turning the chair with his foot against one of the rockers so she faced him.

Her breast was still exposed and he made no move to cover her, instead he tugged the zipper down, exposing her other breast. He placed the second twin in her arms and the baby hungrily rooted around, searching for her nipple. Rocky slipped one large finger under her breast and tugged upward, helping the baby find what it was looking for.

Maggie was breathless, Rocky's touch sending tingles through her body. He'd never touched her this way before, much less seen her bare. Yet she sat there, anticipating his next touch, his next caress.

The back of his knuckles brushed over her other breast, shocking her gaze up to his.

"Are you sore?"

She was surprised by the warmth in his eyes and the care in his touch. He seemed so matter-of-fact. "A little," she admitted. His calm actions made this moment less about embarrassment and more about being cared for. She felt special. Cherished.

"Allie left something for that." He turned away for a moment and she tried to catch her breath, but he was back too soon with a small jar of cream in one hand. When she would have taken it, he shook his head, the dominant streak in his personality asserting itself in a quiet way. "Let me."

She watched, transfixed, as he dipped his finger into the jar and lifted out a small amount of white cream, rubbing it between his thumb and forefinger to warm it before placing the jar on the table at his side. He crouched next to the rocker, putting him on level with her, then reached out with those coated fingers and tugged lightly on her nipple. Soothing warmth spread with his gentle touch, easing the ache while his focused attention started another one lower down.

"Rock—"

"Does it feel good?"

"Yes." Her answer was a breathless whisper as he caressed her abused nipple, sending energy pulsing through her entire body.

"Shifters are more used to nudity than humans," he observed almost conversationally. His touch was that of a caregiver, not a lover, but it still caused thoughts to race through her mind. "We have to get naked to shift, so most of us are used to seeing others in the buff from the time we start shifting."

"But the boys are already shifting," she realized aloud.

"Yeah, it's a little different for bears. Most of the others don't go through their first change until they're in puberty, but bears are more magical than most. Especially these two."

"Because Tony was a shaman?" she asked quietly. Rocky's hand still rubbed the cream on her nipple, but his eyes were focused on hers. They held the soft expression that he reserved for her alone, it seemed.

"A grizzly shaman. That's something special. They say only a snowcat has more magic, and that kind of big cat is even rarer than us grizzlies."

His hand dropped to rest on the fabric covering her thigh and their eyes held for a long, private moment. He seemed to want to say something but was holding back. Maggie broke the connection, looking down to find the second baby asleep in her arms.

Rocky sighed and stood, taking the sleeping baby to settle him in the crib next to his brother. As Rocky turned back toward her, she tried to pull the edges of the robe together, but his soft words stopped her.

"We're not done, Mags." He picked up the tub of cream and repeated the process of dipping his finger inside, then warming the cream between his fingers. He knelt in front of her this time, pushing her thighs wide to settle between them as he rubbed the cream onto her other breast. "Do you know how beautiful you are? Do you know what the sight of you nurturing these babes does to me? Do you know how much I wish I'd been the one to plant them in your womb?" His other hand swept down to cover her stomach, flatter now but not yet back to normal. "I witnessed a miracle last night I will take with me to my grave. Someday, Maggie, I want to see that miracle again, only next time I want the baby coming from your body to be my flesh and blood."

"Oh, Rocky." Her voice trembled, barely heard in the silence of the dark night.

He leaned forward, pressing her back into the chair as his lips covered hers for the first time. But it didn't feel new. It felt right and good, like something she'd been missing all her life she'd finally found. His mouth seduced hers, opening wide and demanding all she had to give, and she gave freely.

She'd loved this man from afar for too long to deny those feelings now.

She yelped when he stood, sweeping her up into his arms. She drew back, her eyes widening as he stepped over to the bed and held her over it.

"I know it's too soon, but I want to sleep with you in my arms. Just sleep."

Swallowing hard, she nodded. He placed her

gently on the bed, shocking her as he unzipped her robe the rest of the way and tugged it off her shoulders. Aside from her panties, she was completely naked as he climbed into bed next to her, wearing nothing but his jeans. He pulled the blanket up over them and drew her into his arms.

The heat of him was exciting and comforting. His skin burned hot, just the way Tony's had, but Rocky was bigger, more solid and a much more commanding presence than Tony had been. Tony had seemed to always hold back with her a little, and she'd realized just before he died it was because she didn't know what he truly was. That last week before his death, he'd let her have all of him for the first time, and she learned what she'd been missing during their marriage.

Tony had always been more cerebral than Rocky. Though Rocky was every bit as smart as Tony had been in high school — both at the top of their class — Tony had been dedicated to more scholarly pursuits, while Rocky excelled at sports and anything physical. Tony could command attention with his words. Rocky did so with his mere presence.

She reached up and kissed his chin as he snuggled her into his broad arms.

"None of that now," he teased, "or we'll never get to sleep." He spooned her from behind, wrapping his arm around her. "I'll give you time. As much time as you need, but you need to understand. You're mine now. The babies need me and I need you, Maggie. As I've always needed you."

"Rocky—" She wanted to ask so many questions, but he stilled her words.

"No. Now isn't the time for talk. We're both worn out and everything is new and strange. We have time now. Time to figure this all out and come up with the best solution for us all. I just want you to know that I'm here for you. I've always been and always will be. That's all. Things will go as slow as they need to go from here." He brushed a tender kiss near her temple, and she suddenly felt the weight of the hours of anxiety and worry lift from her shoulders.

Tony had been magic, but Rocky... Rocky was solid. He was security. He was her rock. Her Rocky.

Within moments, she was deeply asleep.

CHAPTER SIX

The next morning, Rocky woke with an arm full of warm woman and his ears full of the soft sounds coming from the cubs. They were up again, hungry as usual and demanding attention.

Rocky leaned over and kissed Maggie awake— something he'd dreamed of doing almost his entire life. She was more responsive than he would have believed, cuddling into him as he took the kiss deeper.

She'd been through a lot in a short time, but she was stronger than even he would have thought. She'd impressed the hell out of him with the way she handled everything, the way she'd survived on her own with a killer mage on her trail all those months, but the idea frightened him too. Never again would she face danger alone.

"Rocky—"

His breath caught as she whispered his name—
his—as she woke in his arms. Even half asleep, she
knew who held her. The thought sent a bolt of
satisfaction through him that allowed him to draw
farther away. The babies needed them now, but later
there'd be time for the grownups.

"Sounds like Tony and Jim are hungry." He
kissed her chin, nipping slightly. "Probably dirty
too." He rolled out of the bed before he got too
interested in kissing her some more. "I'll help clean
them up, then it's time for a shower. I've got a lot of
work to do today."

Rocky felt a pang of regret for the deliberate
distance he had to put between himself and his
heart's desire. He had to give Maggie time to heal
both physically and emotionally before he pushed her
any further. She needed time to come to terms with
the life he was going to build for her here, in the Pack.
In his home. Starting today.

"Work?" She sat up, clutching his sheet to her
chest. Damn, he loved the way she looked, rumpled
and sleepy eyed in his bed. Where she belonged.

"Some of the Pack is coming out to help me build
an addition for the cubs. They'll need the room as
they grow, and so will we."

He crossed the room, giving each child a good
morning kiss as they quieted for him. They
recognized him already, which boded well for their
future as a family. He set about changing them as he
heard Maggie tug on the discarded robe and zip it up.

"Rocky." Her strong tone made him turn. He had
one of the babies in his arms. "Do you expect us to
live here with you permanently?"

He read confusion and uncertainty in her beautiful eyes. Rocky took a deep breath and placed the now clean, squirming bundle back in the crib before facing her again.

"Yes," he answered simply, stepping forward to meet her troubled gaze. He had to make her understand. "I meant everything I said last night. I claimed these children. They're mine to raise and guide, to love and sponsor through their lives. They need me." He closed the distance between them, grasping her hands as he pulled her forward to meet him halfway. "I'm hoping that at some point you'll need me too. But if you don't, I'll build you your own space, Maggie. Just don't ask me to let you go completely. I don't think I could. Not now."

"I've always needed you, Rocky."

He could hear the unspoken *but* in there and it made him back off, even as her words gave him hope. He'd been bold in declaring his protection for the children and his attraction to her, but he knew she needed time.

Rocky was glad he'd put it out there so she'd know where he was coming from, but he thought it was probably too soon. Too soon to talk about the future. Too soon to consider anything but the next few days. He cursed inwardly, thinking how long she'd been living in fear, not daring to plan ahead, living day to day.

He'd put an end to that. He'd end the threat to her and her children—his children too now. He hadn't been born a grizzly for nothing. He'd protect his new family with everything he could bring to bear. In this case, he had the entire shifter community in this region at his disposal. He'd been living among them for a long time, was one of their community leaders though he had no Clan of his own in the area. He'd helped them all repeatedly. This time, they would help him protect his woman and his young. He knew he could count on them.

Just a few short years ago he'd had no one. But he'd forged his life here with the Lords, and now his decision to live a lone existence among the other Clans—to be surrounded by their family units, but never part of one—was coming back full circle. He had to believe the Lady Herself had guided his steps when he settled here. It so easily could have gone the other way.

Had Tim and Rafe been any other kind of leaders, they may well have driven off a lone bear shifter from their Pack lands. Instead, they'd welcomed him. Made him a part of their extended family. Given him a position of authority within their hierarchy. He would call on that support system now to help him keep Maggie and the boys safe.

But the confusion and worry in her eyes broke his heart.

"Don't worry, Mags. I swear to you, it will all work out."

"I hope you're right, Rock. I'm so afraid." Those last three whispered words made his heart clench.

"Don't be." He stroked her back, folding her into his arms for a comforting hug. He liked the way she fit there, her cheek resting over his heart where it belonged. "I'm here. And there's a big wolf Pack, raptors, cougars and other assorted shifter Clans right outside the door, ready to help protect you and the boys. You came to the right place. Finally."

"I didn't want to be a burden on you and your friends, but there was nothing else I could do."

"Nothing else you *should* have done. Tony sent you to me for a reason. He knew I would protect you and his sons with my life if necessary. I'm only sorry you waited so long to get here."

She stiffened in his arms and he drew back, becoming aware of the babies fussing nearby. He had to let her go. The boys needed attention. But he was reluctant to lose the warm feel of her in his arms. Still, he had time now. Time to convince her that she belonged with him and that he loved her more than life itself. He just had to be patient.

He let her go and they turned together to take care of the infants, the sound of cars pulling up into Rocky's yard drawing him away just a few minutes later. The work crews were here, ready and willing to help him in any way they could. It was a beautiful thing, what Tim and Rafe had accomplished in drawing all the Tribes of the *were* together here.

Rocky, as a strong Alpha, was one of their highest ranked lieutenants, though he never thought much about his placement within the community. He was the only grizzly shifter in the territory, the only one he knew of in the region now that Tony was dead.

Both Tony and Maggie's parents were gone as well, and Rocky's folks had long since moved to the coastal woodlands. They were enjoying their semi-retirement, though he had a feeling once they knew they had grandcubs, they'd be here like a shot. Which reminded him, he had to call today and let them know what had happened. He'd be in big trouble with his mother if she found out through the shifter grapevine.

He went out to greet the work crew, taking his cell phone with him. He'd place the call as soon as he got a moment.

Work on the first small addition to his house was well underway before he had a chance to phone his folks, but he knew he could put it off no longer. Rocky walked a short distance from the house and the new construction and hit the button. Leaning against a tree for support, he waited for someone to answer. He should've known it would be his mother. She always seemed to know when he was calling.

"Hi, mom, it's me."

"Rocco? Sweetheart, how are you?"

Even after all these years on his own, his mother's voice still made him homesick for those early days when she'd baked his favorite cookies and fussed over him and Tony after school. If it wasn't his mom, it was Tony's, since the boys were never far apart as they grew.

"I have news. Can you get Dad to pick up the extension? I think you both should hear all this at once."

"I hope it's nothing bad. Are you all right, son?" He heard her moving through the house as she spoke. Probably looking for his dad.

He heard a click and knew his dad was on the line even before he had a chance to answer his mother's question.

"The news is mixed, but I think overall you'll be happy. First, Maggie's here. Did you know she was pregnant? She had the babies last night. Twins. Twin boys."

"Oh, sweet blessed Lady. Where's Tony? We haven't heard from him in so long, but I didn't worry because he had Maggie." His mother's voice broke his heart. He hated to have to tell her this. Tony had been like a second son to her.

"He's gone, Mom. A mage was hunting him and killed him about eight months ago according to Maggie. She's been on the run from the same people ever since. Tony made her promise she'd come to me when the time came for her to have the babies."

"Twins?" That was his father's gruff voice.

"Yes, Dad. The next Lords, if their appearance at the sabbat is anything to go by. They're already shifting. They've got so much of Tony in them. So much of his magic." Rocky had to swallow hard to keep his voice from cracking.

"You claimed them." His dad's voice was certain. It wasn't a question.

"Yes. They're your grandsons now."

He heard his mother sniffle and knew there were tears running down her face. His dad would probably have his arm around her, offering silent comfort. He hated to have to tell them all this over the phone, but they needed to know.

"We'll be on the first flight we can arrange," his father said in a firm voice.

"Actually, Dad, I'm not sure that's a good idea. We've been up against the *Venifucus* before in recent months."

"*Venifucus*?" His mother's shocked whisper reached through the phone line to twist his heart.

55

Word had gone out from the Lords to all shifters in their domain a few months ago about the reappearance of the organization most had thought long gone. The *Venifucus* were a collection of regular people and magic users intent on bringing back an evil the likes of which this realm had not seen in centuries.

Elspeth, the one known as Destroyer of Worlds, had been banished to a forgotten realm by the combined efforts of many different kinds of magical folk the last time the *Venifucus* had been confronted. Now they were back, and they were trying to bring her back too. It would take a great deal of dark, evil magic to retrieve her from such a place and her minions in this realm were working toward that goal.

They'd already tried to kill Allie and the Lords. They'd failed in that attempt, but who knew how many Others on the side of light had been silenced already? The *Venifucus* were playing the long game, taking out their opposition one by one before anyone even realized they were still a viable organization.

Now that the Lords knew for sure they were back and what they were plotting, the forces of Light were being rallied. Nobody really knew if it would be enough to prevent catastrophe. And no one knew exactly when or how the *Venifucus* planned to act. Vigilence was the order of the day.

"Yeah, that's the other bad news. Tony was killed by a *Venifucus* mage. Another of their mages tried to kill Allie a while back. She's Rafe and Tim's mate, the new Priestess. It was a close thing. Rafe was nearly killed. It took a hell of a lot of magical firepower to get that mage. This one's got to be even stronger. I mean, if he was able to take out Tony..."

It went without saying that Tony was one of the most magical grizzly shamans in recent history. It would take someone equally as powerful or even stronger to take him down.

"All the more reason for us to come out there and help guard our grandsons." Rocky knew that tone in his father's voice. There was no arguing with that particular sound. The old grizzly's mind was made up. Rocky sighed.

"All right. Call me when you have the flight information. I'll get some wolves to pick you up at the airport and bring you to my house. I'm sorry, but I'm not leaving Maggie or the boys for even a minute. I hope you don't mind."

"Mind? Why would we mind? You're doing the right thing. Guard her and the boys. They come first. We'll be fine on our own if you can't spare anyone to get us. We do know how to drive, you know." His mother tried to be upbeat, but he knew it was hard for her. She'd just had a lot dumped on her. It would take time for her to deal with it all, if he knew his mother.

"Don't drive yourselves. You'll be safer in numbers. Until this mage is caught, nobody is running around alone. Rafe and Tim are spreading the word today. I'll make sure you have a strong group to escort you here."

"A wise precaution." Rocky breathed a sigh of relief at his father's easy acceptance of his plan. "We'll call you back with our flight plan as soon as we get it."

"In the meantime, give Maggie and our

grandsons a hug from us," his mother requested tearfully. "Tell her we'll be there as soon as we can."

"I'll tell her. I know she'll be happy to see you."

Rocky ended the call after a few more words, glad to have that ordeal over with. It would be hard when his parents arrived. They'd known Maggie almost as long as they'd known Tony, and they loved her too. It would be a sad reunion without Tony here to share it, but perhaps his parents could help Maggie. They were pillars of strength, and his mother especially might be a good shoulder for Maggie to cry on. Another woman might be able to help with her grief in ways he couldn't.

By that evening, the basic framework of what looked like a whole new house had taken form. Maggie was amazed by the speed with which these people moved. They were not only faster but stronger than normal people, and Rocky was the most powerful of them all physically. She'd watched from the sidelines all day as he hoisted beams and logs easily five times his weight into position while others secured them. The construction was simple and lovely, built to withstand the rigors of time yet blend in beautifully with the surrounding forest as if the home were part of it.

Maggie took the babies outside for a while, setting up a playpen to keep them safe. Various people stopped by to talk with her and coo over them, not blinking an eye when they shifted into little bear cubs, barely able to wobble on their own paws. They shifted twice during the day, each time shocking her a bit before she really took a look and realized how incredibly adorable they were. And their eyes were the same in either form. There was intelligence there, insatiable curiosity and immense and powerful magic.

Rocky scooped up the cubs the second time they became little bears and lay down on the leafy ground with the little ones on his chest. They dug in their tiny paws and made him laugh with their antics as they sniffed at him and licked his neck and hands.

"They are so cute," she said softly.

"Curious too," he agreed, lifting the bear cubs by the scruff of their necks as a mama bear in the wild would have done. It alarmed her at first, but the boys seemed to enjoy the new mode of transport as Rocky placed them back in the playpen. "It's a good thing we'll have this addition done quickly. Soon they'll begin to want to roam, and we can't let them get outside or we'll have a hell of a time trying to keep up with them." He chuckled as the cubs settled down for a little bear nap, wrapped around each other.

Rocky looked at her and she sensed something heavy was on his mind.

"Is it bad news?" she whispered. All day, she'd watched men placing little electronic things all around the existing house. Security lights. Stuff that looked like motion sensors but really small. And after they'd been installed, they were pretty much invisible, even though she knew where to look.

"I called my parents. They're on their way here." Rocky's face was grim, but Maggie's heart lightened at the news. Then she remembered the danger and worry ate at her.

"It's too dangerous. Did you warn them? Do they

know what they're walking into?" She bit her lip, anxiety that was never far away filling her once again.

"They know. Probably better than you do, Maggie." Rocky placed one warm hand on her shoulder and she felt her tension ease a bit. That's all it took. Just that one touch and she felt his strength surrounding her, protecting her.

It was so tempting to just lean on him and let him take over and do everything. She'd done that to this point, and she'd need his help a while longer until she healed fully, but it went against her grain to be so totally dependent on anyone.

Tony and she had been partners in every sense. Or at least she'd believed they had been. He'd been keeping secrets, but that hadn't really interfered with their relationship. They had made all the major decisions together, each respecting the other's wishes and desires. They'd both worked and contributed to the household. They'd shared chores and responsibilities, each taking on what they were best at and pitching in wherever needed.

It had been a perfect marriage. Or so she'd thought. Then one day, out of the blue, Tony had turned into a bear.

A real, live, freaking magical grizzly bear.

"The guys are going to help me move some furniture around this afternoon. The front bedroom is too exposed for you and the boys, but it makes a good guard position," Rocky said conversationally. She looked at the tension lines around his compressed lips and realized he was anything but casual, though she supposed he was trying to keep his words calm for her benefit. "My den is in the center of the house. It's the most secure room in the original structure. You and the boys will be safest there, and I have to make room for my parents. At least at first, they'll want to stay with us, if for no other reason than so they can help with the twins."

While she liked the idea of having help with the boys—especially help she knew and trusted like no other—she worried for the older couple.

"The bad guys will most likely find me again, Rocky. I've managed to escape their notice for short bursts of time, but they always find me. I still don't like putting your folks in danger." The hunted feeling that had plagued her for the past eight months returned in force as she thought about it.

"Honey, we're all grizzly bears. Even though my folks are retired, Dad was an enforcer for the local weretribes near Whitefish. Like I am here. Mom's no slouch either. Never mess with a mama bear, especially when she's protecting cubs." Rocky chuckled. "We're not all that different from our wild cousins, except we have a human side that can be just as deviously clever as those who hunt us. Having three bears in the house—and no Goldilocks jokes, please—will keep you and the boys safe if danger comes to our door."

She chuckled at the Goldilocks line and some of her tension disappeared. Rocky stepped back and removed his hand from her shoulder. She missed the warmth of him, but the attraction she felt for him was still a little uncomfortable. She was Tony's wife. The feelings she'd always had for Rocky were almost easy to ignore when he was so far away, but now that they were sharing space, it was nearly impossible.

"So where will your parents stay?" she asked to change the subject of her dangerous thoughts.

"The front bedroom for now. It's the first line of defense if anyone actually gets past the new security measures and patrols in the woods. My folks can also keep watch from the window in that bedroom. It's got a good view of the front of the property. I'll be watching the back and watching all the new monitors. They can stay there until the addition starts to take shape, and Dad can be a big help with the design."

Maggie knew Rocky's dad had been an architect and builder before retirement, so that made perfect sense to her. She only wished they wouldn't be in so much danger, because she knew in her heart that things had not yet come to a head with the man who'd killed Tony and then chased her all across the country. She feared a showdown, though she fully expected it at some point in the not-too-distant future.

"There will be wolves and other shifters patrolling the woods at all hours, of course. Try not to worry, Mags. There are more resources here than you think. Just because you can't see them all, doesn't mean they aren't here. A large part of our defense is stealth."

She ceded the point, but nothing could make her feel better about the danger on her trail. Danger that she'd brought to these good people who had given nothing but kindness to her and her boys.

CHAPTER SEVEN

That following night—after a day spent watching furniture being moved all around Rocky's house—they had dinner with Tim, Rafe and Allie at Rocky's place. The Alphas, as Rocky called them, explained a bit more about their role as the leaders of all *were*, and the uncommon marriage between themselves and the priestess, Allie. Maggie was shocked at first but tried hard not to let it show. She asked Rocky about it later that evening, but he seemed to take it all in stride, his attitude doing more to settle her mind than his actual words.

He helped her fix the linens on the large bed they'd moved into his windowless den. Some of the Pack members had brought it over earlier in the day. The room was done up in warm, honey colored wood paneling and hunter green fabrics. It felt as much like being in the woods as you could get without actually being outside. Maggie liked it.

The twin sized crib had been moved into the farthest corner, and Rocky had helped ready the boys for sleep as if he'd done it a million times before. Maggie felt comfortable with him at her side helping. Their friendship and the closeness they had always seemed to share had come back to life with very little prodding. He was a steady presence that reminded her of all the good times in her past.

Rocky and Tony had been central figures in her high school years and beyond. That had only changed after her marriage, when Rocky had drifted away and they'd lost touch. She'd been sad but focused on her new life with Tony, and she'd supposed Rocky was forging a new life of his own. She had figured they'd all reconnect eventually, but it hadn't happened. Until now.

"I hope this room is okay. I know it doesn't have a window, but that's actually for the best. It's more secure, and since the boys will probably have you up during the night, the sun won't wake you in the morning and you can sleep in." He looked over at the sleeping children. "If the cubs will let you."

She nodded in agreement, smiling at the babies now fast asleep in their crib.

"It's perfect." And it was. Close to the bathroom and centrally located in the house, she could see how it would be the safest place for the boys.

Rocky's massive desk, a state-of-the-art computer setup and several filing cabinets had been taken out to make room for the bed. Rows of built-in bookcases held everything from adventure novels to stock market analysis. The crib, a changing table and the rocking chair had been arranged on the far side of the room from the door. All in all, it was very homey for something so makeshift.

Rocky and his friends had moved out all the furniture, but hadn't been able to do much about the books. She didn't mind. She liked books and would probably spend some time browsing the titles if she couldn't sleep.

"We're going to do some more rearranging tomorrow. The Pack will be out early to help, so don't worry if you hear a bunch of trucks pull up in the drive just after dawn."

"I'm sorry to have brought such upheaval to your home." She was amazed at the way he'd taken all of this in stride.

He turned and caught her in a quick hug. "I'd do anything for you, Maggie. Moving a little furniture around is the least of it," he whispered near her ear and kissed her hair before releasing her.

He'd been treating her with kid gloves since that first night. He'd backed off, which both confused her and brought comfort. Her emotions were all over the place, and she wasn't sure she could have handled full on seduction mode from him on top of everything else. Knowing Rocky, he was sensitive enough to realize it and was cutting her a break.

"If you need anything, just call. I'll be in the living room tonight. Right next door. If nothing else, I can help you juggle the twins if and when the boys wake in the middle of the night. Mom and Dad are flying in tomorrow and the wolves will bring them from the airport about mid-morning. After that, you'll have all the help you need with the boys. We should also have a bit of the new construction done soon, so we'll have room for everybody and everything."

She knew his computer had been set up on the coffee table in the living room. His desk and the other furniture from the den had gone into the construction zone and sat under a tarp.

Things were up in the air in many ways, but in the way that mattered most—the security of the babies—she felt more confident than she had in a long, long time. They were safer here with Rocky and his friends than they would be anywhere else. In the back of her mind, she knew the bad guy on her trail would have to be dealt with, but she was letting things ride for now. Trouble would come for her sooner or later, but this time she had powerful allies. This time she wouldn't run. She would make her stand here, with Rocky.

The next morning, Rocky made pancakes for breakfast. It had been a long time since anyone had made breakfast for her and she appreciated the gesture.

"My parents should be here in about an hour," Rocky said conversationally as they ate together. The boys were asleep in a playpen they'd set up in the living room, with a baby monitor on so Maggie could hear if they stirred.

Maggie felt conflicted by the idea of Rocky's parents coming to help. On the one hand, she wanted to see them and bask in the warmth the older couple had always generated. On the other, she couldn't bear facing them knowing she had brought such bad news about Tony. She had failed her husband in so many ways. If she'd been a shifter, maybe he wouldn't have died.

Why he hadn't felt able to tell her about being a grizzly shifter until his final days only drove home to her how much she hadn't known about Tony. And about Rocky. And about both of their parents. She'd been living in the dark, blissfully unaware of the dangerous existence these people faced every day. She'd been such a fool.

"It'll be good to see your parents again." It was the right thing to say and she felt the truth in her words as she spoke them. Still, she couldn't kick the feeling of having been less than Tony needed. If not for her human limitations, Tony might still be alive. It was a staggering thought that had hounded her steps from the moment she'd left their burned out home over eight months ago.

"I know they're looking forward to meeting the twins." Rocky's grin was infectious as he looked over at the babies, now crawling all over each other in bear form. "My mom will likely spoil them rotten. Dad too, though he'll never admit it."

"I always loved your parents. They were so welcoming when we were kids. And after I got engaged to Tony, I realized just how close they were to him."

"They loved him as a second son. When his parents died, they claimed him, though he was really too old for a formal claiming. The families had formed a close bond being the only two grizzly shifter households for hundreds of miles. We formed our own little Pack, and for a while it was really, really great."

"You miss them." She stated the obvious but he didn't seem to mind, lost in thought.

"Every day. It's not often that weregrizzlies have the opportunity to bond in such a way. We're a rare species and somewhat solitary, so most families live on their own, raising their cubs one by one."

"Sounds lonely."

"It can be. But it's the nature of the beast to want to prowl solo. I've had to temper some of my loner tendencies to get along with the wolf Pack. It's been worth it though. I like belonging, even if I'll always be a bit of an outsider because I'm different from the rest of them." He grinned. "Of course, that comes in mighty handy at times too. Few, if any, of the other shifters will stand up to me. Makes me helpful to the Lords as an enforcer."

"You said that before. What exactly does that entail? I've been wondering how a grizzly bear fits in with a wolf Pack." She was learning so much here.

"Well, you know I'm an engineer by trade. I work for one of the Pack's companies. Mostly, I work from home, but once in a while I have to go into the office or visit a client's site. That's my mundane job. On the shifter side of things, I'm a lieutenant in the hierarchy headed by the wolf Lords. Since they rule all *were* on this continent, their organization encompasses many different kinds of shifters. All the Allied Tribes, anyway. So it's not that strange for me to be included in their chain of command. Now if it was just a wolf Pack, I doubt they'd want me anywhere near. But Rafe and Tim are special."

"So are you." She smiled at him, loving the way he'd taken charge of his life and found a place for himself in this strange world she was only just beginning to understand. "I'm sorry to have to come here and complicate your life, but I want you to know I'm grateful you took me and the boys in and that you're willing to help combat the danger that's been following us." She would have said more, but he silenced her gently with one upheld hand and a rueful look.

"There's no need for gratitude between us, Maggie. I don't want you to ever feel beholden to me for doing something that comes as naturally as breathing. Caring for you and the boys is part of me. It's something I do without conscious thought. I hope one day you might feel the same connection I've always felt for you. And Tony. And now his sons. My sons." Rocky swallowed hard and she could see emotion in his warm gaze.

She was saved from answering as they both heard another car pull up in the gravel drive. Rocky stood and went to the window, glancing at his watch. The mixture of chagrin and consternation on his face was easy to read.

"Are they early or are we running late?" She carried their plates to the sink and began to neaten up the kitchen.

"Both," he said on a gusty sigh. "I'll go get their luggage. Looks like they're planning to stay a while judging by the bags tied to Pete's roof rack. Good thing he took the SUV to get them."

Maggie followed him out of the kitchen and through the house, hesitating at the front door. But when she saw Rocky's mother hop out of the SUV, she found herself sprinting toward the older woman.

Within moments, she was wrapped in a warm hug as tears streamed down her face.

Maggie hadn't had motherly support for far too long. She'd lost her own parents a few years back. It was a loss she still felt every day — particularly since she'd become pregnant.

"Mrs. Garibaldi, it's so good to see you." Maggie pulled back when she was able to force her emotions into a semblance of order.

"Just look at you, Maggie, dear. You're still as beautiful as you were when you were a girl. But so sad." Rocky's mother touched her cheek, turning with her toward the house. "We'll work on that. But first, I want to meet my grandbabies. And you must call me Marissa now."

Maggie hastened her step. She'd left the children alone in the house. Embarrassment flooded her cheeks along with anger at herself. She didn't think. She was a bad mother.

Relief flooded her system when she saw the boys were sleeping soundly in bear form in the playpen. They were wrapped around each other like little bear cubs sharing warmth and they were the cutest babies she'd ever seen.

Marissa Garibaldi seemed to think so too. She cooed quietly to the boys, careful not to wake them up as she smiled down at them.

Maggie heard Rocky and his father enter the house and place bags down on the floor in the front bedroom. The men joined them and Rocky stood behind her as his dad took his place behind his wife. The love between the older couple was so obvious and so real it made her ache for what she'd lost.

After a moment of admiring silence, the older couple preceded them out of the room and into the kitchen. Rocky's dad gave Maggie an unexpected hug that knocked the wind right out of her and made her want to laugh at his exuberance. He was as big as his son, with sparkling brown eyes that spoke of his merry, easygoing nature.

"It's good to see you, Maggie. It's been too long," he said as he let her go.

"I've missed you both," she admitted. "It's been a rough couple of months."

That statement sat out there like an eight hundred pound gorilla until Mrs. Garibaldi took her hand and gave it a compassionate squeeze.

"Rocco told us all about it. The important thing is we're here now. The family is all together and we protect our own. You'll be safe now."

God, she hoped that was true. She didn't want to bring down any more sorrow on these good people.

Marissa Garibaldi took over the kitchen and soon scrumptious aromas were wafting through the house. Rocky's dad went off with him to the construction zone, to meet the Lords and consult with the Pack members who were helping build the addition to the house. Maggie tried to make herself useful cleaning and straightening up while she kept an eye on the twins, now back in human form. She fed them and changed them, enjoying the idle time with her boys as she got to know them both.

The men came back for lunch and were joined by what looked like at least half the work crew. Mrs. Garibaldi served up a spectacular meal while Maggie helped by distributing plates and utensils and making room for all the extra people to sit. She felt a little superfluous, but she was still moving slower than her normal pace, her energy returning at a more human rate without the magical assist from the boys, which had worn off for the most part after that initial burst of healing.

Marissa insisted that Maggie nap after they'd cleaned up from the lunch crowd. She was so weary she didn't resist the idea too strenuously. She woke when the boys did, to feed and change them before she sought her own dinner.

Rafe, Tim and Allie joined the Garibaldis for dinner and were soon discussing events and politics that were well beyond her rudimentary grasp of shifter society. It was okay though. Rocky sat next to her and tried to explain what he could so she could at least try to learn.

"Marissa and Joe," Allie spoke during a lull in the conversation. "We want you to know that you both are welcome here anytime."

"And if you wanted to relocate here permanently," Tim picked up the conversation, "you would be a very welcome addition to our community."

Silence reigned while Rocky's father regarded the three who ruled over all the other *were* in North America. Even Maggie could tell this invitation wasn't given or received lightly.

"We are honored," Joe Garibaldi answered after a slight hesitation. "We haven't made plans yet, but it's something to think about."

"We'd like to be near our son and help raise our

grandcubs," Marissa added. "But we're not sure yet how everything will work out."

"Of course." Rafe smiled to cover the slight tension Maggie sensed swirling around her.

The Garibaldis were being so nice. It was clear they didn't want to presume, and saying anything right now would be awkward.

Maggie would never deny her babies the gift of knowing others of their kind, and she would have to corner Rocky's mom later and reassure her on that point. Maggie might not be too comfortable with the idea of people turning into bears—and all other kinds of dangerous wild animals just yet—but she'd have to adapt, for the boys' sake.

"Let me help you bring in the desert, my dear." Joe turned the subject handily while the main course drew to an end. The older couple stood and headed for the kitchen.

"Your parents are great, Rocky," Allie was the first to comment.

"Thanks. And thanks for making them welcome. My dad's a stickler for propriety so he really needed the invite from you to be sure he wouldn't be perceived as invading your territory. I'm not sure they'll take you up on the offer though."

"It would be a nice change," Joe's deep voice sounded as the older couple rejoined them. He was carrying a pie in each hand and his wife held another.

Maggie was still amazed by the vast quantities of food these people could put away. Lunch had been huge and dinner likewise.

"So you'll really think about it?" Rocky seemed pleasantly surprised and a bit eager.

"Yes, we will," his mother answered, sliding a giant piece of blueberry pie onto his plate. "There's nothing much in California for us. Not when you consider that the babies are here. It's been too long since we had cubs to spoil."

"I told you they'd spoil them rotten." Rocky rolled his eyes in exaggeration as Maggie laughed.

CHAPTER EIGHT

The Garibaldis moved in, and though the men didn't discuss it in front of her, Maggie figured out that they'd set up some kind of sleeping rotation so that someone would always be awake and on guard in the house. Every time she woke up with the boys, no matter what time it was, day or night, either Rocky or his dad were just outside her door, in the living room, keeping watch.

She slept late the next day and managed to join the Garibaldis while they were still at the breakfast table discussing plans for new construction. Rocky kissed her good morning. It was an innocent kiss, just a buss on the lips really, but it still made her blush. His parents no doubt noticed, but didn't say anything.

"How are the boys?"

"Sleeping again."

"Enjoy it while it lasts," his mother advised. "They'll be little balls of energy soon enough, and with two you'll have a hard time keeping track of them. I remember how it was with Rocky. Until we pooled our resources with Tony's parents, each of us were having trouble keeping up with our boys individually. It'll be easier here in the woods with so many other shifters around, but the little ones could still easily get into trouble when they start to roam."

"Which is why we're discussing these plans." Rocky's gesture invited her to take a look at the drawings still spread on the table.

It was another house, very similar in style to Rocky's growing cabin, but definitely different. And they were professionally done. Very slick with measurements and calculations along the borders.

She gazed up at the elder Garibaldi. "Did you do these, Mr. Garibaldi?"

"I think you're old enough to call me Joe now, don't you, Maggie?" Rocky's father winked at her and smiled, though it felt strange to think of him by his first name. "I couldn't sleep last night so I went out and prowled around. There's a beautiful spot right nearby — close enough for safety and far away enough to give you a little privacy. We could build there easily and the position would be very defensible should anyone or anything threaten the boys."

"We'd be nearby to babysit whenever you needed it," his mother added with a smile. "We could connect the yards so the boys would have plenty of room to prowl but still be in a safety zone as they get older. Between Rocco and Joe..." she patted her husband's arm, "...they would be well protected."

"Wow." Maggie sat back and took it all in. "You've certainly thought this through."

"We want to help you, Maggie," Marissa said kindly. "We've always thought of you as one of the family. Since before you married Tony. You're home now, among friends. If you let us, we'll protect you and the boys. But if you feel like we're overwhelming you, we'll back off."

"No," Maggie was quick to clarify. "Oh, no. If anything, I'm overwhelmed that you're so eager to help and so accepting of me when I'm not...like you. Not a shifter, I mean." She blushed but Marissa's sparkling eyes put her at ease again. "I'm not saying this well. I'll admit it's confusing and a little scary to go from being all on my own to having you and Rocky and all those wolves willing to help us. I'm just trying to take it all in and realize that we're safe—or as safe as we can be—for the moment. Believe me when I say, the last thing I wanted to do was bring danger to you, but I've been running from Tony's killer for months and it's more than I can handle now that I have the boys to consider. I don't know what I would have done if Tony hadn't made me promise to come here. As it is, I feel bad for sticking you with my problem."

Rocky put his big arm around her and drew her to his side as they both sat around the kitchen table. He was such a comforting presence.

"None of that, Maggie. You should have come right away. I can't believe you ran all over the place with a murderer on your trail. You're more resourceful than I thought, but it ends now. Now we're a team. United against anyone or anything that would threaten you or the boys. All right?"

His big brown eyes dared her to disagree, but not in a threatening way. She knew he had her best interests at heart. He loved her—if she dared believe him. Maggie nodded and gulped back the emotion that threatened to escape.

"All right."

"Good." Joe looked pleased. "So then what do you say to grandparents living nearby? Would you mind having us around?"

"Are you kidding?" Tears spilled down her face as she looked at Rocky's parents. They'd always been so kind to her. So welcoming. She knew they'd be good for her boys—and her—if she let them into her life. There was no doubt in her mind on that score. She reached across the table to take Marissa's hand in hers. "I'd love to have you here."

"So you're definitely staying?" Marissa asked.

"I'm not too proud to admit I need help with Tony's killers still on the loose. Once they're dealt with? I don't know exactly where I'll live yet, except that it'll be somewhere in these woods so my boys can grow up where it'll be safe for them to be what and who they are. Even though I'm not like you, I've felt very welcome here, and I know my boys would do well with such good people all around. Everyone here has been so helpful."

Marissa sighed. "I'd hoped—" she began, but cut herself off from whatever she'd been about to say. "Never mind. Things will happen as the Lady wills. For now, I'm just glad you realized the twins need their Alpha." She smiled at her grown son. "We all need those little boys and we'll be ready to help you raise them, watch over them and teach them about being grizzlies whenever you, or they, need us. You've made a good decision to raise them here."

They talked about building plans until the work crews showed up. Rocky and his dad went out to meet them, toting the new plans with them.

Between the fussing of the twins, the whirlwind of construction, Rocky's mom helping Maggie sort out being a new mom and the danger she felt approaching, Maggie was worn to a nub over the next week or so. She floated in a limbo of uncertainty and frantic activity while the house started taking on its new shape and some of the interior finishes were being tackled. Rocky asked her advice on colors and designs, which made her feel part of the new building in a way she hadn't expected.

The boys would eventually have their own room, right next to a giant master bedroom on the second story of the new part of the house, but that wouldn't be for a while yet. For now, she was enjoying the makeshift den/bedroom and Rocky's extensive library. She'd made use of it often when the boys woke her up and she couldn't get back to sleep right away.

Time passed quickly with everything remaining carefully obscure between Rocky and Maggie. A status quo of sorts had been reached, though he was insinuating himself more and more into her life. He was her helper at all hours with the boys and always seemed to be there when she needed him.

One memorable night, Rocky again helped her with the middle of the night feeding. He soothed one twin while the other nursed. He changed them and talked to them in a rumbly whisper that seemed to set them both at ease. They fell asleep again with little fuss.

"Thanks, Rock," Maggie whispered, standing next to him as they gazed down at the sleeping babies.

She and Rocky had learned to work as a team over the past weeks. Maggie wasn't getting enough sleep, but Rocky was there even when she felt most like a zombie. He didn't talk much, moving silently around the room to make her life so much easier. He cared for the boys as if they were his own flesh and blood, and she watched him wistfully at times, wondering if Tony would have been half as attentive to his sons as Rocky was.

Tony had been less hands-on than Rocky in many ways, though he'd done his share of the chores in their home. Tony had been sort of half in this world and half in the next most of the time, his head in the clouds, thinking profound thoughts. He didn't seem to know exactly where clean laundry came from, except to occasionally show his appreciation.

Not that Tony had taken her for granted. Far from it. But he'd had important work to do that she hadn't always understood…or known about, for that matter. He'd traveled a lot, and sometimes had clients visit his office, but she'd never really understood that many of those so-called clients were shifters in need of his unique abilities and counsel.

Tony guided many shifters in esoteric matters that she'd known nothing about until the very end. She'd seen some of the few records he'd kept before she torched the lot. She'd burned everything according to his wishes, keeping only a small portable hard drive that held the work of his lifetime and some videos he'd made for his sons. Several terabytes of irreplaceable data that was her burden and her gift to their children and his people.

She didn't know why she hadn't given it to Rocky yet, but the burden felt heavier every day. Maybe now was the time to release it.

"Rocky, there's something you should look at. Something I've been carrying with me since Tony died." She turned away from his questioning gaze and went to the pocketbook that still held her most prized possessions.

She dug through it to the hard part on the bottom where she'd secreted the drive inside the lining of the bottom support piece to protect it. It was wrapped tightly in plastic and she was glad to see it had come through its ordeal in good shape as she handed it over to Rocky.

"What's on it?" He seemed to hesitate as his hand touched the casing she held out to him.

"All of Tony's records, plus some videos he made for the boys. I'll want those backed up to something I can carry in my bag. Along with the folder labeled *Private*. Everything else is yours to disseminate where you think it should go. There's probably some stuff on there relating to other shifters Tony was helping that might be best in the hands of Allie or the Alphas, but you should decide. You know more about this world than I do." She kept her voice low so as not to disturb the sleeping babies, but they showed no signs of waking.

"Why are you giving this to me now?" Rocky's hand closed over the drive still in her hand, engulfing both in his gentle grip.

"It seemed the right time. I'm sorry I didn't do it before now, but it just never came up, and to be honest, for a while there I'd pretty much forgotten about it. So much was happening and there was so much to get used to. I'm sorry, Rocky. I didn't mean to hide anything from you. It's been my burden for almost a year now. I guess I wasn't quite ready to share it yet." Her own words took her by surprise and made her pause.

Had she been holding on to the past, even unconsciously? Was this last link with the life she'd had with Tony more symbolic than even she had realized?

"But you're able to share it with me now?" He stepped closer, his deep voice sending shivers down her spine.

A feeling of freedom caught her off guard. She lifted her head so she could meet his gaze. She'd been staring at their hands while she spoke, but she felt lighter now somehow. Braver.

"Yes, I think so. Maybe."

She tilted her head and smiled at him, not really sure of her own feelings. But she was certain of one thing. Something more momentous was happening here. A sea change of some kind was just beginning. It was a slow start, but it was definitely a start. Where it would lead, she didn't really know, but she was willing now to at least try to find out.

Rocky smiled in return, just a little, and it touched her heart. He was so serious all the time, making plans at all hours with the other shifters regarding security and the ongoing construction. All that in addition to his regular duties for the Lords and his engineering work. She'd caused a huge disruption in his life, but he never complained. She would take some of the burden from him if she could.

"I like it when you smile, Maggie mine. You don't smile often enough these days."

"I smile all the time at the boys," she protested as he took possession of the hard drive and placed it in his pocket. He didn't let go of her hand, using it to draw her closer.

Her breath caught as he tugged her nearer. A new excitement was in the air. A brand of electricity that she'd felt from time to time when Rocky touched her or looked at her in a certain way, but he hadn't pressed her response, and for that she'd been grateful.

No more, though. Now, she was willing to at least try to see where this shivery feeling might lead. Maybe.

Still uncertain, she allowed him to pull her into his arms.

"You smile at the boys," he said softly near her ear as he tucked her into his embrace. "But you don't smile at me."

"I'm smiling now," she teased, trying to lighten the serious mood as she rested her cheek against his chest. She loved the way he felt against her, so strong and sure.

"Really?" He drew back so he could look at her face. She kept the smile on her lips even as he lowered his head and reached tentatively for her mouth with his.

Oh, yes. This is what she wanted. The taste of him. The feel of his arms around her, his warmth wrapping her in his strength.

When she wanted more, he gently set her back. "Not too much, my heart," he warned her in a whisper. "I don't want to ruin this by asking for too much, too soon."

He rested his forehead against hers, rocking her in his arms from side to side in a slow, soothing motion.

"Thank you for trusting me," he went on a few minutes later. They'd been holding each other in silence, just enjoying the moment.

"I trust you with everything that's most precious to me, Rock. My life. My boys."

"Everything but your heart," he said in a soft whisper that made her want to deny the truth of his words, but she knew she was still holding back.

Her heart had been broken by Tony's death. It would take time to heal. Time before she could trust it to Rocky's care. If she dared take that big a risk again. At this point, she still didn't know if she was brave enough.

"If I were to give my heart to anyone again, it would be to you," she admitted, knowing the truth of her words deep in her soul.

"Thank heaven for that, at least," Rocky replied with a small grin. "Don't worry. I'm not rushing this. I'll take what you can give, when you're ready to give it."

"You're a special man, Rocky." She kissed his stubbly cheek, loving the masculine feel of it against her lips.

He let her go and left the room on silent feet, leaving her standing and watching him disappear back into the other room. She felt something monumental had just happened but she couldn't put it into words.

She stood watching the doorway for a long moment. Finally, she turned to her bed and settled down to sleep with a soft smile on her lips and the warmth of Rocky's arms a pleasant memory.

CHAPTER NINE

One afternoon, Allie showed up with what seemed like a truck full of groceries to help replenish the larder. Thanksgiving was only a few days away and Marissa was already planning a feast.

Different wolves from the surrounding Pack had been helping keep the cabin stocked with supplies, but this was the first time Allie had been back since those first days. Marissa invited her in and the three women spent some time putting things away and then chatted over coffee.

Maggie enjoyed getting to know Allie better. She was a lively woman with a surprising background. Maggie learned that Allie had been raised in the human world, with no knowledge of shifters, though she was related by blood to a bunch of cougars. She'd been just as shocked as Maggie when she'd first learned about the whole society that was hidden from the rest of the world.

Allie stayed and helped them cook dinner since her mates would be joining them to discuss the expanded building plans. When the babies started fussing, Allie and Marissa shooed Maggie out of the kitchen and suggested she take them outside for a little fresh air.

Maggie liked the idea. She'd been cooped up in the cabin for a while and wanted to see how the building was progressing. Each day she heard the sound of saws and hammers, but she hadn't seen much of what the men had been doing since that first outing.

She stepped out the front door, lugging the dual baby carrier someone had donated — most likely Tim and Rafe. The boys waved their tiny hands and feet happily as they felt the fresh air on their faces. They loved the outdoors, just like their father had. Like Rocky did.

Thinking of him, she wasn't surprised to see him hefting a giant log into position on the side of the house. They'd had to clear a bit of snow the past week to get to the construction area, but the men were making judicious use of tarps and plywood to keep the snow out of the newly constructed areas. Eventually they'd break through the kitchen wall to join the new section on to the existing structure. It looked like that would be much sooner than she thought. These shifters moved fast.

Maggie walked nearer the work zone, careful to stay a safe distance, but Rocky saw her almost immediately and came over.

"How's my favorite girl?" He leaned down to

buss her cheek, making her feel all tingly. He smelled good. Like man, hard work, pine needles and fresh air. It was a heady combination.

"Your mom and Allie talked me into taking the boys for a little walk." She looked down at the carrier and Rocky bent to take the heavy burden from her. He lifted it like it weighed nothing at all, while she knew firsthand that it had to weigh a good twenty to thirty pounds with the boys in it.

"A brilliant idea," he agreed. "Want to see the progress we're making on the addition? We'll be ready to break through into the kitchen any day now. Maybe even tomorrow."

"Really? I had no idea you were that far along." She walked with him as he strolled toward the work area. She noted he was careful to keep clear of any place there were people actively working, instead taking them through a side entrance where it looked like things were mostly finished for the day.

"We move fast on tasks like this. A lot of our people work in the construction industry. Some of the best building companies in the country are owned and manned by shifters of various Clans and Packs."

"Really? I guess that makes sense, since you're naturally so strong and agile."

"Plus we really like to work outdoors and build things in harmony with nature."

"You've done that here. This addition really blends with its surroundings. And it's huge. I didn't realize you'd intended to build quite so much on to your house."

"Well, it isn't just me anymore. I've got two boys, who will grow into big fellas, and you to consider. A small cabin was fine for a bachelor, but I always wanted a big house if and when I had kids to worry about. Grizzlies need space to roam, even inside their dens."

"So then you really want us to stay with you? I mean permanently." She was nervous about his answer.

"I told you before, darlin', I intend to raise these cubs. I want them with me. I want you with me, but it's your choice. You can live here. You've seen the plans. You can have your own suite if you want it. I won't force you into anything more intimate." He placed the carrier down on the floor next to him as he strode forward to face her. "Not unless you want it too. I can be patient." He tucked a strand of hair behind her ear and gave her a lopsided grin. "At least I can *try* to be patient."

Her breath caught as he took her in his arms. She saw his kiss coming a mile away but didn't try to duck. She wanted his lips on hers, wanted his warmth, his strength. The future was still uncertain, but for now she needed his caring, to know that he was here for her, willing to put up with her indecision and hesitancy…and fear.

The kiss went from comforting to blazing hot in two seconds flat. Rocky's big arms contracted, drawing her into his strong body. She felt buffeted by his heat, his maleness. Safe and protected. She was also turned on. Rocky could kiss like no one had ever kissed her before—with a desperation and desire that answered something equally needy inside herself.

Sex with Tony had always had a dreamlike quality. Something soft, gauzy and sensuous. She'd loved that about him. But Rocky's raw, primal energy was something new and thrilling. Just kissing him made her feel womanly and almost...wicked. Like a temptress.

She felt powerful. Like she was in charge, and yet not. Like she held the key to his pleasure and it was up to her whether or not she allowed him any. Maggie had always been more like the girl next door than the femme fatale, but Rocky made her feel like Mata Hari and Helen of Troy, with a little Lara Croft thrown in, all rolled into one.

The bang of a car door somewhere outside drew them apart. They were both breathing hard as Rocky looked deep into her eyes. He released her by slow degrees, visibly struggling to get himself under control. She felt the same.

"I'd better see the work crew out. They put in a big day today." Still his gaze held hers as if reluctant to leave.

One of the babies hiccupped and broke the spell. Rocky moved back and released her arms.

"Will you three be okay here for a minute? It's safe. We've beefed up the perimeter defense so nothing should be able to get to you as long as you stay near the house."

She nodded, unable to speak for the moment. She was still recovering from that killer kiss.

He walked off and Maggie took the time to really look around at the interior of the building. It was going to be gorgeous when they finished it, and it was well on its way to completion. Even though the insides of the walls were still exposed, showing where they were in the midst of putting in plumbing and wiring, she could see the skeleton of what promised to be a beautifully airy but functional structure.

She liked what she was seeing. In one corner on top of a stack of wood was a rough drawing of the plans she'd seen a few weeks back. So much had happened since then that she didn't remember much of the detail and found herself intrigued by the handwritten notations that looked like they'd been added over the past couple of weeks. Things were changing as they went along—for the better, it looked like.

The architectural details that were being added were lovely and the handwriting was familiar. Most of the notes were in Rocky's bold hand. A few others were in his father's handwriting. All were slight improvements on the original rough design and made the place even better, in her opinion.

She studied the drawings for a while, getting lost in daydreams of how it would be when it was finished.

"I see you found the plans," Rocky spoke, breaking the silence, derailing her reverie. He looked lovingly uncertain as he approached her. "So do you want the grand tour? Everything's been secured for the night so it's safe for you and the boys."

"I'd love to see what you've done so far." Touring the newly constructed addition was a safe activity. Safer than picking up where they'd left off with that tempestuous kiss.

Rocky lifted the carrier with the boys in it and led her outside again so they could begin with an overview. He pointed out the way the yard would form an L-shape with the new addition and the rest of the house.

"You can see the yard from the kitchen window this way and from the windows on this side of the addition, so we can keep watch on the boys later when they play outside. And my folks are going to build on the other side, so we can all keep watch over them. I'm going to move my den to that room on the end there. Dad suggested we put in a bay window and skylights on that end because he knows how I like the natural light. This time I'm building the office to suit me, rather than making do, but we'll leave finishing that 'til last since the other parts of the house are in more immediate need." He moved them toward the addition once again, escorting her in through one of the openings covered by a tarp where a door had been framed but not yet put in. He pointed to the far wall. "We got the windows on that side done today. Tomorrow we'll do these."

As she went into a different room this time, she realized the work had progressed to an amazing degree. This part was closer to the existing house and was nearing completion. The walls had been put up, electrical outlets and fixtures had been put in and windows and doors had been fitted. Paint was up on the walls and gleaming hardwood floors peeked out from under protective drop cloths.

"My folks can move out here after Thanksgiving. We'll have heat in here by then and we'll have broken through from the kitchen so they can easily access the rest of the house. We wanted to finish a room for them so they wouldn't have to be cramped into that front bedroom anymore. It's really too small for two adults. Eventually, this space can be converted into a formal dining room, if you decide that's what you want."

He took her through the rest of the addition, which was probably twice as big as the original house had been, pointing out the various rooms. There was a play room for the boys and bedrooms for them as they grew older. There were additional bathrooms and a living room that would house computers and an entertainment system, he said, as well as that gorgeous office space at the end of the house just for Rocky. It was all beautiful, efficient and well crafted.

Maggie was in shock. That anyone would be able to not only design but build a substantial part of such a great place in a little less than a month simply amazed her. It felt as if Rocky had been planning this for years—though she knew there was no way he could have known she'd show up when she did. Still, he had dived into the project with both feet and seemed genuinely excited about what his house had become—and *would* become—in such a short time. He was building a *home*. Someplace the boys could grow up and belong. A place they could always come back to even after they were adults. A place that would endure.

The thought touched her heart and she found it difficult to speak, impossible to express her thoughts on such a momentous feeling.

"I decided to keep the master bedroom suite somewhat separate from the rest of the addition. The walls and floor will be sound proofed with the master bath on one side and walk-in closets on the other. I figured the kids would pretty much dominate the place as they grow, but we can always hide in the master suite for a little privacy."

She sucked in air at the implications of his words and the heat in his eyes. He stepped closer, lowering the boys' carrier to the floor once again as they paused in one of the larger rooms.

"I'd love for you to share it with me, Maggie. Eventually...if you want to."

His voice rumbled through her, igniting her senses once more. Rocky could do that so easily to her — set her on fire with a few simple words. But it was too soon. She didn't know what she really wanted. She didn't trust that he really wanted her.

Rocky had always been too darn noble for his own good. She couldn't be certain if he really wanted her or if he was doing his *duty* to Tony by taking her in and protecting her. She'd take the protection. She wasn't foolish enough to believe she could handle the threat to herself and the boys alone. But she wouldn't commit to a relationship where she was a consolation prize at best, or at worst, an obligation.

"I don't know, Rocky — "

He silenced her protestations with his lips, pulling her in for a continuation of that amazing kiss from before. She was reeling with sensation as he swept his tongue into her mouth, swept his hands downward to cup her rump and pull her against his lower half. He was aroused.

That knowledge sent a thrill of pleasure through her. She'd done this to him. Maggie Hobson had made Rocco Garibaldi hard.

Damn, that was a sizzling thought. For so many years she'd watched him and dreamed about him.

She never thought he'd ever see her as more than a little sister.

She'd loved Tony with all her heart, but somewhere in the back of her mind she'd never forgotten Rocky. Her first crush. The star of her childhood dreams. And now she was in his arms, sharing an adult kiss complete with straining bodies, a hard cock and a wet pussy that wanted him inside in the most delightful, dangerous way.

She wrapped her leg around his thigh, then higher to his hip. He was so huge and solid, so reassuring and totally hot. If she were honest with herself, she'd admit she'd wanted him for a long, long time. But all conscious thought fled as Rocky moved his skillful hands beneath her sweater to touch her ribcage.

He'd held her in his arms before, but she'd been too uncomfortable both physically and mentally just after the twins were born, to really enjoy the sensations. She was healed now physically, and each day helped her come to terms with her new situation. She felt every brush of his calloused fingers against her sensitive skin as he moved cautiously higher, climbing her ribcage in slow increments.

She moaned when he cupped her breast. The soft fabric of her bra was the only thing between his warm palm and the yearning, aching tip that wanted so much to feel his possession. But he was careful with her. He touched her as if he knew how exquisitely sensitive and sometimes painful her nipples were now that she was nursing.

Rocky was attuned to her body in a way no man had ever been. He touched her, squeezing gently as his other hand palmed her ass, keeping her close to his hard erection. His kiss went on and on, delving deep, claiming and coaxing, demanding and giving.

Until the babies cried.

The first little wail entered her consciousness. Rocky lifted his head immediately and it registered that he was looking downward, but it didn't occur to her what he was doing right away. She felt drugged. Lethargic and needy. Her mind didn't want to come back from whatever blissful plane of existence Rocky had sent her to. But then the babies' cries reached her brain and she pulled away with a gasp.

She had to untwine her leg from around Rocky's pillar of a body, embarrassment flooding her cheeks as she realized just how far gone she'd been. Rocky looked at her worriedly, seeming torn between taking up where they'd left off and the boys.

Hiccupping cries seemed to decide him. He bent to the carrier and checked the boys. He was such a responsible adult. While she felt more like a horny teenager than ever before.

She watched him, trying to gather her wits and slow her rapid breathing. If they'd been in a car, there would be fog on the windows from the steam they'd generated. How Rocky could function after such a devastating experience was beyond her, but thank goodness he could.

She'd chastise herself later for being a bad mother, but for this moment, she was glad he was here to see to the boys. She wasn't quite sure if she'd have been able to think rationally enough to do it at the moment.

"They're okay. Just wet." He stood with the

carrier over one arm. "We'd better go in."

CHAPTER TEN

Neither of them spoke of the interlude, but when Maggie fell asleep that night after a boisterous dinner with Rocky, Rafe, Tim, Allie, Betina, Marissa and Joe all crowded into Rocky's house, she had troubling dreams. She didn't sleep well. The pattern of her nights prior to arriving on Rocky's doorstep had returned.

Things were chasing her in the dark of her dreams. Things with hideous, evil faces. Not ugly. No, far from it. These things were beautiful in their evilness and very appealing. They cajoled and teased her even as they tried to lure her into their trap, but she was strong. She had to be. For her babies.

Maggie woke in a familiar cold sweat the next morning, noting that Rocky had apparently come in at some point and taken the babies into the living room. She could just see them in their carrier through the door he had left cracked open. Smart man, he'd realized that she would worry if she couldn't see the boys the moment she woke up.

They made a cute picture, the three males. Rocky was staring at his laptop screen, occasionally sparing a loving glance for the babies who rested in their comfy carrier at his side. Both the laptop and the big carrier were positioned on the long coffee table in front of the couch on the far side of the living room, in line of sight with the door to the room where she slept.

He must have traded the use of his more powerful desktop computer for the laptop's portability so she could see them immediately upon waking. His thoughtful gesture brought a smile to her lips even through the echoing memories of those horrible dreams.

She got up and went to the door as quietly as she could. Rocky heard her the moment the blanket rustled, of course, but said nothing. The babies were sleeping, looking angelic.

"Do I have time for a shower?" She spoke as softly as she could, knowing Rocky would figure out what she was saying. He had super sharp hearing. Unfortunately, so did the boys, and she really didn't want to wake them until she'd had a chance to calm down from those horrendous nightmares.

He looked down at the babies, then up to her and nodded with a concerned smile. This was a departure from the routine they'd established. Normally, she wanted to cuddle her sons the moment she woke up, but today was different and there was no hiding it from Rocky.

But she couldn't go near Rocky yet. Not now. She didn't have time or the inclination to discuss her nightmares with him before she'd had a chance to wash away the sweat that clung to her skin. She'd have to ask Rocky if fear really did have an odor. Maybe it was for the best that she didn't get too close to her babies if they could smell the terror that had filled her dreams. She didn't want to upset them—or Rocky.

She wanted to be strong for all three of the males. She wanted to be as strong emotionally as their bear side was physically. It was a tall order, she knew, but she'd been strong for the past ten months. She could be strong a little longer. That was her mantra, and if she repeated it enough she might even begin to believe it.

Maggie grabbed a few items and headed for the bathroom. Fifteen minutes. Just fifteen minutes of cleansing hot water. That's all she needed now to make her ready to face the bears waiting for her out there again.

Twenty minutes later, a freshly washed and dressed Maggie joined Rocky in the living room. The babies woke as she entered and sent up those cranky sounds that she'd learned preceded outright wailing. Without a word, she took them back into the bedroom and closed the door. This once, she wanted to care for them herself, without Rocky's help.

About a half hour later, she opened the door to the living room once more. The babies were back in their carrier, dozing lightly. She took them with her as she left the bedroom.

"Is everything okay?" Rocky asked in a gentle, soothing tone she was certain he cultivated for the benefit of the babies. His eyes squinted in concern as he met her gaze.

"Yes and no." She sat on the sofa a few feet from him, placing the boys' carrier back on the coffee table. "Rock, I had awful nightmares all night long." She studied him to see if he understood the seriousness of her pronouncement, and it was clear he didn't get it. "I've had nightmares off and on since Tony died, usually right before a close call with the jerks on my trail. The dreams are warnings." She smiled and shook her head. "I never would have said something like that a year ago, but I've learned the truth of it. The dreams come when danger draws near."

Rocky's brows lowered and she was glad to see he was considering her words carefully. He stood and started to pace. Well, for a mere human it would have been pacing, for him it was more like stalking silently around the room. She noticed that he went behind the babies' carrier so they wouldn't be able to see his agitation. Smart man. Her little boys were very observant for one-month-olds. Of course, they were half grizzly bear, so nothing about them was as it would have been with purely human babies.

"Are you sure about these dreams?" He paused in his prowling to ask.

"Yes. I think our respite is about to come to an end and the nightmares are a warning." She hated the thought of it, but as she spoke the words she knew in her heart that they were true.

"I'm glad the Lords and the priestesses will be here for dinner. This is something we need to discuss." He ran one hand through his hair in a restless gesture. "Will you be okay to talk about the details of the dreams? Betina might be able to interpret what you're seeing, if you're willing to describe it."

Maggie swallowed hard. "Yeah, I can talk about it. I don't really want to, but if it could help, I'll do it."

Rocky returned to her side and took one of her hands. "I'll be there. You can always lean on me, Mags."

Dinner was quiet but nice. Rafe, Tim, Rocky and Joe talked about Pack business and told amusing stories about some of the youngsters who were getting into mischief. Betina and Allie spoke with Marissa and Maggie about the dinner and other trivialities until after dessert was served.

But there was a feeling in the air...as if they all knew there was something important hanging over their heads. Maggie felt it most of all. She knew they were going to ask her about the dreams. She wasn't looking forward to it, but knew it had to be done. They had to know what she had seen and maybe — just maybe — they would help her figure out what in the world it all meant.

"I hear you've been having nightmares," Betina finally broached the subject as Marissa cleared away the dessert plates.

Maggie took a deep breath before replying. "I've had them before. Every time danger got too close to me, or the killer had found some sort of clue to my whereabouts, the dreams started up. I came to realize they were sort of an early warning system, giving me time to relocate and hide my trail as best I could."

She saw that she had everyone's attention. It wasn't as uncomfortable as she'd imagined it would be. These were all friends. They would help her and her babies.

"What kind of dreams?" Betina asked gently.

"I'm being chased. That part is pretty straightforward. But the thing that's chasing me is grotesquely beautiful. No, that's not the right word. I'm not really sure how to describe it. It's absolutely stunning. Gorgeous. And wholly evil. So evil its beauty becomes ugly. If you're just looking at its outer shell, it would be very easy to trust. But underneath, evil radiates from its core. Palpable, pulsing waves of evil. I don't know how else to describe it."

Betina's eyes narrowed in concern and Maggie noticed everyone else around the table had varying expressions of unease, though none showed any fear.

"Is it a creature or a human?" Tim asked.

"Sometimes it's human. Sometimes it isn't, but I can't see the actual shape. I think it has horns and it's surrounded in a swirl of red. Red and dirty brown. Black." She tried to recall the images from her nightmare. "It's like a sickly miasma of evilness. Dull and dirty. Like bloody mud."

"A demon," Betina announced after a brief pause.

"I knew nothing mortal could take down our Tony," Marissa said after a long moment filled with stunned silence.

"Damn, Mags. You've been running from a demon for the past nine months?" Rocky seemed impressed and a little horrified.

"I always knew our Maggie was made of sterner stuff than most humans," Joe said approvingly, giving her a little wink of encouragement.

"The dreams always warned me when to move," she explained.

"So we've got a demon in league with the *Venifucus* coming here." Tim boiled the situation down to the bare facts. Rafe let out a low whistle between his teeth. Nobody looked pleased at the idea.

"We'll lose the outer perimeter guards if we don't pull them back," Rafe said, sitting back in his chair. "They're the youngest and least experienced of our fighters," he explained, probably for Maggie's benefit.

"Then pull them back," Betina said swiftly. There was a decisive air about her. "This is not something that can be fought solely on the physical plane. I fear this is a job for Allie and I. And Maggie," Betina nodded toward her, shocking Maggie speechless.

"No." Rocky shot up from his chair, clearly agitated. "There's got to be something I can do."

"Oh, there is Rocco." Betina smiled at him and he seemed to calm down. "This evil thing must be fought on the spiritual plane by us women, but you can deal with the body that presents itself in your front yard."

"You've seen something, haven't you?" Rocky asked as he took his seat again, calmer now.

"I didn't know what it meant until just now, but I think you'll get the fight you want, and it will be out there..." She gestured toward the front of the house where there was a small clearing in addition to the gravel drive. "And you will wear the heartstone to protect you from its magical assault," she announced.

"When?" was Rocky's only question.

This one Maggie could answer. "Not for a few weeks yet, judging by my experience. But if I'm going to fight instead of flee this time, we all need to prepare. I don't want anyone been caught off guard. The evil in this thing is unlike anything I ever could've contemplated. I don't want anyone to die—and especially not be killed by this demon—on my account."

"Forewarned is forearmed," Tim agreed.

"Don't worry, Maggie," Rafe put in. "Now that we know what we're up against, we can formulate a better plan."

They left it at that and Maggie's heart was a little lighter now that the problem was out in the open. Even better, Betina had given her a name for the faceless danger that had plagued her dreams for so many months.

After that momentous evening, the day before Thanksgiving dawned bright and clear and the work crews showed up early. This was the day they were planning on joining the newly sealed addition to the main house. All the windows and doors had been completed the week before, along with heating ducts and electrical wiring.

The plan was to join the two halves so work could continue inside. Rocky's parents would be the first to try out the addition, moving into the large guest room that had been prepared for them. It wasn't entirely finished, but it would do.

The mood brightened when the hole was cut. The men cleaned up as they went, so that by the time they left at around three o'clock, the kitchen was clean and ready to use. Marissa took over then, organizing a celebration dinner for the family. She'd already sent every man on the work crew home with a pie she'd baked the day before, in addition to the big fresco luncheon she'd served.

The woman was in her element cooking for the crew. Maggie remembered how Marissa had always enjoyed entertaining and throwing parties back when Rocky and she were kids. It seemed like Marissa was really enjoying the opportunity to cater to so many hungry shifters.

The family spent the evening admiring the newly expanded kitchen and adding little finishing touches. Maggie mostly watched, keeping an eye on the boys while Rocky and his dad moved things around at Marissa and Maggie's direction. Before long, the place looked as if it had always been as big as it was now. Seamless. That's how good the construction was, even if it had been accomplished at record pace.

When it came time to prepare Thanksgiving dinner the next day, Maggie helped as much as she could. The men had disappeared somewhere and she had the boys with her in their carrier as they worked in the kitchen. Maggie made green bean casserole and a few other side dishes while Marissa took care of the really hard stuff. They chatted and talked about old times, holidays past and what Maggie could expect as the boys grew.

It was the kind of talk Maggie missed. Her own mother had been gone for years now, but she still missed her every day. Marissa's presence helped fill that void a little. She was a part of Maggie and

Rocky's shared past that brought back only the best memories of childhood and her teenage years. Maggie also trusted Marissa implicitly. She was a good person, with high moral values and a kind heart. She'd be a terrific grandmother to the boys as they grew.

"We're lucky we've had a warm autumn," Marissa observed. "We can work in all kinds of weather, of course, but things are always easier when you don't have three feet of snow to contend with." They both laughed.

"I guess it gets pretty snowy up here," Maggie observed looking out the window. It was already dark.

"The henge of stones at the top of the hill radiates magical energy downward that probably protects this area from the worst of the weather. But shifters tend to like the cold. Our bodies run hot naturally and the fur coat can get a little too warm in the heat of the summer."

Maggie kept forgetting that all the Garibaldis were grizzlies. Even petite Marissa. She hadn't seen anyone actually shift form except Tony, but that had been enough to impress her. She wasn't sure she wanted to encounter even sweet Mrs. Garibaldi when she was in her *fur coat,* as she put it.

Maggie was saved from answering because they heard the men stomp in the front door just then. She set the table while Marissa set out the platters of steaming meat and side dishes. Rocky and his dad appeared a few minutes later, still dusted with a fine layer of snow in their hair.

"Snow flurries are getting thicker. Might have an

inch or two by morning," Joe reported as he swooped down to kiss his wife's cheek.

"Where've you been?" Maggie asked, curious.

The men shared a secretive smile before Rocky answered her question. "Just getting some fresh air." He pulled out her chair at the table and moved the boys in their carrier to a small table within reach. They'd decided to eat in the expanded kitchen as a way of christening the addition to the house. They'd added a leaf to Rocky's big table so that it straddled the wide opening that led to the new part of the house.

Rocky sat next to Maggie and his parents took their places opposite, the table nearly groaning under the weight of the platters of food Marissa had insisted they needed. Maggie knew by now that shifters ate a lot, but she doubted three of them plus her could even make a dent in the feast they'd set out.

Joe reached out and took one of Maggie's hands. Rocky took the other and Marissa completed the circle before Joe spoke.

"The holiday season that begins today is a special time for the world. We celebrate the birth of hope, the Mother's blessing on Her people. This year, we also celebrate new additions to our family. We welcome them and love them for the hope they bring to us." Maggie felt a tear in her eye as Joseph's words struck true. He winked at her and she gave him a teary smile. "May we all continue to live in peace with nature, in harmony with our spirits and in safety from our enemies."

As blessings went, it was a beautiful one, if a little strange. Maggie hadn't known Rocky's father could be so eloquent. He's always been a man of few words around Maggie when she was a girl, but she was learning so much more about Joe Garibaldi now. He was the rock upon which his family leaned. His son would be the same for her sons, she had no doubt.

Dinner brought back good memories of the holidays she'd spent with her mom and dad and then later with Tony and his parents. The Garibaldis had many of the same traditions and included her in them naturally—from playing tug-o-war with the turkey's wishbone to the luscious mince pie served for dessert.

Maggie enjoyed herself immensely and the boys provided entertainment by shifting to grizzly form halfway through the meal and wriggling around until they'd freed themselves of their diapers. Maggie had to repair the damage as soon as they changed back to human form, grateful there hadn't been any accidents while they were uncovered.

Joe was grinning from ear to ear when she turned back to the table.

"They held their shift longer this time," he said directly to Rocky. From the expression on his face, Maggie assumed that meant something good.

"Longer each time, from what I've seen," Rocky agreed, also grinning. "And no issues changing back. They'll really be something when they get a little older."

Joe gave her a challenging look. "Do you think little mama bear can handle it?"

She felt the teasing air in his words and didn't take offense. "I think so. As long as they don't start biting."

Everyone laughed, as she'd hoped. They lingered

over coffee and she was reluctant to see the evening end. But the men had a surprise in store. They ushered everyone into the living room and Maggie stopped on the threshold.

"A tree. You got us a tree."

A gorgeous, seven foot pine tree stood on one side of the big room in front of the picture window. Several new boxes of lights sat on the chair that had been moved aside to make room for the tree. Rocky motioned her over and handed her one of the small boxes.

"Rafe got these in town when he went down for groceries. I don't have many ornaments, but at least we'll have lights."

"It's perfect." She went up on tiptoe and placed a kiss on his cheek. "Thank you, Rocky."

Joe cleared his throat dramatically. "I helped too, you know. Don't I get a kiss?"

Laughing, Maggie gave Rocky's dad a big hug and a peck on the cheek. "Thank you both. This is the best present ever." To her surprise, emotion clogged her throat for a moment, but she mastered it.

"Shall we trim the tree?" Rocky asked, smiling so kindly, she knew he understood how touched she was by his gesture.

"Oh, yes. Then we can sit in here with just the lights from the tree. I always used to love that when I was a kid."

"I remember." Rocky leaned in and kissed her cheek in a simple gesture of affection that almost brought all that emotion back to the surface.

"You two set up those lights. We'll watch the fire and keep an eye on the boys." Marissa said as she sat on the couch by the crackling fire her husband was tending.

The twins were deposited next to Marissa who fussed over them while Joe finished with the fire and sat back in an easy chair beside the couch. Rocky turned to Maggie and helped unwrap the new sets of fairy lights. Together they wound them around the tree. Rocky handled the highest branches, moving things around at Maggie's direction as she stood back. Then she moved in to help with the lower branches that were within her reach.

They worked well together, and within about twenty minutes the tree was lit with twinkling multicolored lights that brought a smile to her face. In fact, she didn't think she'd stopped grinning since walking into the room.

"This was so thoughtful of you, Rocky. Thanks." She turned to him and looked up into his handsome face.

He moved closer and put his arm around her shoulders, standing with her to admire the work they'd accomplished on the tree. A quick peek at the older couple told her Joe was napping—or pretending to nap—and Marissa was fully engaged in admiring the babies. Maggie felt a pang in her heart for the people in her life who could have—should have—shared these moments but were now gone.

"This is my first Christmas without Tony," she whispered, snuggling into Rocky's protective embrace.

"I know. Mine too. Even if I didn't see him, we talked on the phone every holiday. He made it a point to track me down around this time every year."

Rocky hugged her close and warmed her with his comfort.

"I didn't know that. I'm sorry, Rock. I wish I'd known about you all sooner. It hurts to think he didn't trust me enough to tell me until it was almost too late."

"He couldn't take the chance that you'd reject him, Maggie. He loved you too much," Rocky said quietly. The words touched her soul.

"I wouldn't have rejected that side of him. It would have scared the crap out of me, but I like to think I would've accepted it even without the pressure of being in danger. I know I would have. Especially knowing that you and both sets of parents were shifters too. That calmed me down almost right away. I mean, I've known all of you for so long. My parents really liked your families. They were ecstatic when I got engaged to Tony. There was never anything weird or sinister about any of you. After the initial shock, those memories of your families comforted me."

"You always were a reasonable child." Marissa's voice came to her from just a few feet away. Joe stood beside her.

"We're turning in," he announced. "It's been a long day and I'm looking forward to sleeping on that new bed."

Maggie smiled and went to him. "Thank you for the tree, Joe. Happy Thanksgiving." She gave him a peck on the cheek.

She hugged Marissa, wishing her a good night as well, and the elder Garibaldis left them alone with only the boys as chaperones. Which is to say, alone, for all intents and purposes. One glance told her the boys were sound asleep.

Rocky saw his parents out and turned off the lights on the way back to her, leaving just the tree lit with a warm glow. She'd always thought the little lights gave off a magical blend of color that harmonized into a homey feeling.

"Shall we sit by the fire?" Rocky took her hand and led her toward the roaring blaze.

Instead of the couch, where the boys slept in their carrier, he sat on the floor and pulled her down beside him. They used the couch as a back support and sat on the thick, braided rug that fronted the fireplace.

Rocky put his arm around her and she snuggled into his side as the light from the fire and tree splashed over them. Both warmed her in different ways, as did the big man at her side. She felt more comfortable with him, yet on edge. The tension between them rose as the flames licked at the wood, his presence licking metaphorically at her insides, making her yearn for something she was afraid to reach for.

There'd been so much tragedy in her life lately. She was so afraid she'd brought more to Rocky's home. She didn't want to lose him. And she really didn't want to be the reason he was in danger, but that couldn't be avoided now. If the danger found her, it would find her with Rocky because she couldn't leave him now.

"Have I told you how thankful I am that you took me in when I arrived unannounced on your doorstep?" She rested her head against his shoulder as they looked at the flames.

"I'd never turn you away, Maggie. Not ever." The warmth in his voice made her shiver.

"But you could've been married with a family of your own. You should've been." She drew back to look up into his eyes from close range. "Why didn't you marry, Rocky?"

"The only woman I wanted was already taken." Her breath caught at the look in his eyes. "I didn't want to settle for second best. I figured I'd live my life alone. Seemed better than making some poor woman miserable simply because she could never be you."

This time she did gasp. "Are you serious?"

"Darlin', most shifters know their mate when they meet them. I was too young to really recognize it at the time, but the first time I saw you, I knew you were special. It was some time before I figured out you were my mate. For me there is no other woman but you, and there never will be."

He didn't give her a chance to respond as he lowered his head and locked his lips onto hers. But she didn't mind. His admission was shocking...and thrilling at the same time. Maybe life did give second chances.

Rocky loved the feel of her in his arms. The warm fire in front of them, the soft glow of the fairy lights on the tree and the hot woman in his arms combined to make him feel almost lightheaded with wonder at the joy that had come out of tragedy. Maggie was in his arms, at last, and that erased all that had come before. At least for the moment.

"I want you so much, Maggie. Say yes. Let me

make you mine." He stopped his headlong rush with effort, knowing he had to give her a choice. He also had to say what was in his heart. She had to know all of it before she made her decision. "I've always loved you, Maggie mine. Always."

"You have?" Her expression was so hopeful it touched him deep inside.

He nodded. "I love you, Maggie. I want you to be my mate, my wife. I've loved you since I was a teenager, but I never knew how to tell you."

"God, Rocky," she whispered. "I love you too."

She reached over and kissed him, wrapping her arms around his neck. Rocky took her down to the soft, braided rug and rolled so that she was underneath him. She moaned in agreement, never letting go of him. She seemed as hungry for him as he was for her and had no fear of letting him know it. He loved that — and so many other things — about her.

But his Alpha side demanded submission. Slowly, he levered himself over her and pressed her downward. "Bare your neck to me, Maggie. Show me you're mine."

CHAPTER ELEVEN

The growl in his voice turned her on like she'd never been turned on before. Maggie looked up at him, reading the need for her in his gaze, the power of him evident in every line of his body. This was the man she'd loved most of her life finally claiming her. And this *was* a claiming...body and soul. She could feel it.

A little hesitantly, she bared her neck, stretching to the side while trying to hold his gaze. She saw him smile and noticed his teeth were sharper than human teeth were supposed to be. Rocky's grizzly traits were a little more obvious than Tony's had been. She jumped a bit, but this was Rocky. She knew in her heart he would never hurt her.

He growled low in his throat. The sound warmed her, sending spirals of warmth roiling through her body. Rocky's head descended and he nuzzled her neck, scraping his teeth lightly over her skin. It should probably have hurt, but she felt nothing other than excitement and yearning.

"Rocky, *please*." Her whispered plea seemed to energize him.

He lifted her top over her arms and did away with her bra in almost the same motion. She'd almost gotten used to him being around when she nursed the boys, but this was different. He knew what she looked like and how tender she was, but they'd never really crossed the line into all out passion. They'd flirted with the idea a few times, but they both knew this time he wouldn't stop.

She wouldn't stop him and she'd kill him if he tried to call a halt. No, this time they were going to see their mutual attraction through to the end. Rocky's hands went to her pants, unbuttoning and unzipping her with little fuss. She helped him as he pushed the pants and panties down her legs and kicked them away.

Then he levered up enough so he could unzip his jeans. She worked on the buttons of his shirt, not wanting any cloth between them. She had it open only moments before he pushed his jeans down. He took a moment to put on a condom, which touched her deeply. He hadn't needed to be asked. They hadn't had to discuss anything. He knew what to do without being asked. The action spoke louder than words about his care for her.

He returned, sheathed, to rest his hard cock against her naked core. She was hot, wet and ready for him, and she wanted this like nothing she'd ever wanted before.

"It's got to be fast this time, Mags. I'm sorry for that." He nipped at her earlobe, his teeth sending shivers of delight down her spine. "But I promise I'll make it up to you for the rest of our lives."

"Do it now, Rocky. I can't wait either." She shivered in his arms, wrapping her legs around his waist, silently urging him to take her.

Never had she been so ready so fast. But she'd been waiting for Rocky for years. She'd waited long enough.

He hesitated just one more moment more before pushing home, long enough to watch her expression as he moved inside her for the first time. The moment was filled with magic, frozen in time and filling both hearts with the joy of homecoming.

"I love you, Maggie."

Rocky seemed to lose control then, pounding away at her body as if he would never get enough. He stroked inside her long and deep, fast and powerful, and she wanted it all.

"*Rocky.*" Her pleasure was uttered in a broken whisper as a tumultuous orgasm broke over her senses, but he just rode her through it, bringing her higher still. The second time she peaked, she gasped at the pleasure, sharp, intense and so amazing she didn't know if she would ever come back to earth. But Rocky pushed her higher yet.

The third time she came, she raked her nails down his back, scratching him as he bit into the tendons where her neck met her shoulder, not breaking the skin, but placing his mark of ownership there for all to see. Maggie didn't mind the small pain. In fact, it enhanced the experience, drawing a low moan of pleasure from her this time as Rocky came hard and fierce with her.

When the storm eased for them both, he rested his forehead against hers as he rolled them to their sides. His cock stayed semi-hard within her as if he didn't want to leave now that he'd finally been granted access to her body.

"You're amazing, Maggie mine, and I love you with all my heart."

She stroked his slick skin gently, wrung out after the intense love making. "As I love you, Rock."

They got up a few minutes later to clean up and check on the babies, but the boys were still fast asleep. Rocky joined her in the bedroom and made love to Maggie again, slower this time. He let her ride at first, then switched positions, taking her from behind while she moaned in pleasure. Maggie had never had so many orgasms in so short a time, but she wasn't complaining. Her werebear lover was insatiable, and she loved everything about him.

The next day, it was impossible to hide the change in their status from Rocky's parents. Marissa and Joe were all smiles and knowing winks and Maggie knew she blushed a few times by the heat scorching her fair cheeks. Rocky seemed to take the teasing in stride, though he was also happier than Maggie had ever seen him. He took every opportunity to touch her, stroking her hair as he passed her chair, taking her hand as they sat side by side.

And he was smiling a lot. More than he'd ever smiled before. Each and every smile touched her heart, knowing she was responsible—at least in part—for putting that joyful expression on his face.

Come to think of it, she was smiling a lot too.

"Why don't you two take a walk?" Marissa said after lunch. "I'll look after the cubs, and Rocco can show you a little more of the mountain. You must be tired of being cooped up in this house all day."

"Great idea, Mom," Rocky grinned, kissing the top of his mother's hair as he passed her. "Want to do a little sightseeing, Mags? We'll stick close to the house, within the security perimeter."

Maggie liked the idea of being alone with him. She hadn't been away from the babies since they were born, but she knew Marissa would keep them safe.

"I guess it would be all right. And I'd like to see more of the area around the house. I haven't gotten to see much except the driveway and what I can view out the windows."

"Great." Rocky took her hand and led her toward the hall closet. "Allie gave me a parka for you since she didn't think you have much cold weather gear when you got here. She also sent along gloves and a scarf, I think."

Rocky kitted her out in short order and they left, heading for the woods. Rocky led the way, showing her paths she hadn't really realized were there. They weren't marked, but once she knew what to look for the pathways were a little easier to spot. The one he took her on first led from his house out a ways and down the side of the mountain a little.

"That's the Lords' house. Allie, Tim and Rafe live there," Rocky pointed to a lovely building set in the woods farther down the trail.

A smaller trail branched off from the main one they were on, leading down into the Lords' front yard, but Rocky didn't take it. Instead, he led her onward toward a destination only he knew.

He stopped a few times to point out neighboring homes, but he stayed on the main trail that led around the side of the mountain and slightly downward. Finally, he took one of the smaller trails that branched off from the main and they entered a stunning forest glade. One minute they were in the cold sun, the next they were in a warm, shaded, almost magical spot that was filled with all the colors of green, from light to dark. Growing things defied the winter outside, prospering in this small, protected glade.

"Betina's house is through there." Rocky pointed to a small trail marked with bursts of color. On closer examination, Maggie realized they were red berries on holly bushes growing on either side of the trail.

"But what I wanted to show you is right through here." Rocky lifted a trailing vine so Maggie could step under.

She stopped short. Beyond the sheltering vines, there was a pool of water fed by a trickling waterfall that sent cold water into what must have been a hot spring beneath. Steam rose from the pool, causing a mist to cover the ground. The warmth seemed to be held in by the surrounding greenery, which was much more lush than the winter world outside.

The warm steam that drifted out of the grotto made this protected spot comfortably warm in an otherwise cold, wintery world. For the moment, they'd left winter behind and found a pleasant space between seasons, beyond time. A space where they could be together in a stolen moment, away from their cares and worries.

"It's like a little oasis of summer in the middle of a cold world," Maggie whispered, feeling as if this place was sacred somehow.

"That's a good description." A new voice caused her to turn sharply. Rocky was right behind her, but the new man spoke from off to her left somewhere.

"Stop skulking, Slade. Come out and meet Maggie." Rocky's tone was friendly, even teasing, so she took her cue from him and relaxed a bit.

The man who stepped out of the leafy cover to their left was one of the most exotic beings she'd ever met. He was as tall as Rocky and just as muscular, though built on the leaner side. He looked sleeker somehow. And more deadly.

"Honey, this is Slade. He's in charge of security on the mountain."

"Pleased to meet you, ma'am." Slade nodded and smiled slightly, but it didn't help him look any less dangerous.

His black hair shone with health and vitality. His blue eyes seemed to dance in amusement when he realized she was struck speechless by his abrupt appearance.

"Don't let him scare you, Mags. He's on our side, thank the Goddess."

"Oo-rah," Slade commented quietly, and both men chuckled. "If there's anything you need, you know where to find me, Rock."

"Thanks, buddy. For now, I'm just giving Maggie the nickel tour. Tim and Rafe filled you in?"

"You know it," was his cryptic answer. "We're as ready as we can be."

"Good. Thanks for helping with this."

"It's my honor." The expression on Slade's face went from humor to seriousness in the blink of an eye. He stepped forward and lifted Maggie's hand. She'd apparently been struck dumb by the man's presence. Why couldn't she think of anything to say?

"Your cubs will be safe here, ma'am, if I have anything to say about it. They're the future. Thank you for bringing them here." Slade bowed over her hand and sniffed once, then kissed her knuckles lightly.

It was an odd gesture, but she figured it had to mean something among shifters. Maybe he was learning her scent for some reason? Maybe that would help him protect her babies? The idea intrigued her and she knew she'd have a bunch of questions for Rocky when they were alone again.

She nodded, still not speaking to the strange man. He confused her senses and made it hard to think of anything to say that wouldn't sound rude. So she kept silent. He seemed amused again as he let go of her hand and turned to leave. Between one blink and the next, he was gone.

What in the world was he?

Rocky was chuckling when she turned to look at him. She hit his shoulder.

"Stop laughing."

He laughed even harder. "I don't think I've ever seen you speechless before."

"Well..." She didn't know what to say to that. He was right. "There's something odd about that guy."

"You could say that." Rocky's chuckles subsided but the smile didn't leave his face as he drew her into his arms. "Slade's a tricky one. Ex-military, like a lot of our best warriors, but there's something about him even spookier than most of the Special Ops guys."

"You can say that again."

"There are all kinds of rumors about his origins," he went on conversationally, stroking her hair away from her face.

"What rumors?" She grew breathless as the look in his eyes mesmerized her.

"Do you really care?" He drew closer, lowering his head to tease her lips with his. "Slade isn't the man for you." He moved his mouth to her neck, making her shiver.

"I know." She gasped as Rocky's teeth teased the sensitive skin behind her ear. "You are, Rock."

He growled and bit down on her earlobe gently. The sensation went straight through her, making her yelp in surprised pleasure.

"I'll never get enough of you, Maggie mine." His lips found hers again and his kiss was an assault of the senses that she welcomed.

Nothing else existed for her but this man, this moment, this loving embrace. She was surrounded by him, enveloped in his passion and she wanted to give him all she was and more. She felt her heart open up, as it did every time Rocky was near, and pour out love for him.

He popped the snaps of her parka open as he moved her backward and pinned her to the trunk of a wide, sheltering conifer. The scent of pine surrounded her, making her very aware of the untamed feel of the setting and the way the man who kissed her fit so well in this wild, sacred place.

Rocky unbuttoned her shirt and pulled down the cups of her bra to cup her bare breasts in his big hands. They were sensitive, but he knew just the right pressure to use to make her squirm with arousal.

Maggie let herself bask in the moment, enjoying every touch, every exciting caress. She'd never made love outdoors before, but she had a feeling that was about to change. She'd never been so daring in her life.

Rocky dipped his head to her neck, grazing his slightly pointed teeth over her sensitive skin in a way that made her moan.

"That's right, honey, let me hear how much you want this. We can be as loud as we want out here. The babies won't hear." His words were gasps against her throat as he slid his hands lower, lowering her pants with impatient, arousing motions that drove her wild with desire.

She'd had to be so careful not to scream his name when he took her before. She'd wanted to, but there had been the sleeping children to consider, not to mention his parents. But out here, in the secluded grotto, it almost felt as if they were the only two people in the world. Sure, that other very disturbing man had been here, but he was gone now, disappeared into the sheltering trees, and the feeling of being locked away from everything and everyone was pervasive. Maggie let her spirit rise to Rocky's challenge and would not hold back this time.

No, this time was for them alone. No children. No parents. Only the two of them alone in the woods that were Rocky's natural habitat. It seemed fitting that he make love to her here, taking her in that special place in the light of day and the presence of the tall, protective trees.

Maggie toed off her sneakers, helping Rocky rid her of her pants and underwear. They made a nice pile of insulating fabric to stand on, but Rocky probably wouldn't leave her on her feet for long.

Maggie's hands went to his waistband while Rocky's mouth returned to hers, the fire between them flaring hotter and higher with each second that passed. She unbuttoned and unzipped to find him bare beneath his soft jeans. He didn't seem to like underwear, and that was fine with her at the moment. One less barrier to what she wanted.

Rocky broke the kiss and reached into the pocket of his shirt. His jacket was open, but his flannel shirt was still buttoned, rubbing enticingly against her nipples when he kissed her. He produced a foil wrapped condom from the shirt pocket and ripped it open with his teeth.

She'd never seen anything sexier than his impatience. Maggie took the condom from him and rolled it onto his thick cock, caressing him as she did so, loving the way he growled when she squeezed him.

"Any more of that and this'll be over before it starts, Mags." He swooped low to put his hands under her bottom and lift.

He was so strong, he lifted her as if she weighed nothing at all. The parka she still wore protected her back from the rough bark of the tree as Rocky slid her upward. She wrapped her legs around his waist when he had them aligned.

Rather than the quick claiming she had expected, Rocky held her gaze with great solemnity as he directed his cock into her waiting, eager pussy. He slid in, inch by inch, watching her expression, his eyes saying more than words ever could about the specialness of this moment.

When they were fully joined, he paused, continuing to hold her gaze.

"You are my heart, Maggie. My soul. My whole life. I would die if I lost you now." She saw the stark truth of every single word written on his rugged face. "Please say you'll never leave me."

"I won't ever leave you, Rock. Not voluntarily. You are my home," she answered simply. It was a truth she felt down to her toes. Finding him again. Being with him... She had finally come home.

Rocky's eyes filled with emotion and he leaned forward, sealing their declarations with a brutal kiss that aroused her even more. He pinned her against the tree with his body and began to move in long, languid motions that made her pant and gasp, moan and sigh. She even growled a few times when he took her to the precipice of pleasure, only to back off before she could tumble over.

Their lovemaking was primal. Eternal. Rough and wild, just like Rocky. She loved it. She loved him.

And this time, she did scream his name when he made her come.

"I hate to interrupt something so obviously enjoyable," Slade's voice came to Rocky from behind. He'd known the damned cat shifter hadn't really left.

Maggie gasped and fought to be let down. Rocky complied, lifting her off him and lowering her feet to the pile of her clothing still on the ground at their feet.

"It's okay, honey. He can't see much of anything," he whispered, then lifted his head, directing the rest of his words to the sharp-eared cat. "And if he comes any closer, he's going to have one very angry bear to contend with. Damn your hide, Slade. Can't you see we're busy?" Disgust filled his tone, but it was tempered by amusement as Maggie tried her best to hide against his chest.

"They need you back at the house and I was asked to escort you there. There've been some developments."

What the cat wasn't saying got Rocky's attention. Nobody had ever needed to *escort* a full grown grizzly shifter anywhere. There must be danger in the woods and the damned cat was trying to tell him there would be safety in numbers. For Maggie's sake, Rocky agreed.

"All right." Rocky tried to sound nonchalant, but all his senses were on alert. "Go wait outside the grotto while we get decent. We'll join you in a minute."

The moment Slade slinked off into the woods, Maggie crouched to retrieve her pants. She shook them out before sliding into her panties and pants, then shoved her little feet into the sneakers she'd kicked off before. She was moving fast and her color was high. She was cute when she was embarrassed.

"I can't believe we were seen." She sounded shocked as she concentrated on the knot of her shoelaces.

Maggie had taken a seat on the soft pine needles beneath the tree. Rocky wanted to join her, but he dared not be caught on the ground. He knew there was danger in the woods, thanks to Slade, and he wouldn't let his guard down again.

"It's not that bad, Mags. He really couldn't see anything, except maybe your ankles and my butt. And thankfully, Slade doesn't roll that way." Rocky had to chuckle at that thought as he pulled up and zipped his pants. "It's not uncommon among shifters to be caught naked in the woods. It's natural for us, more or less. Not something to get upset over. I'm sure he's seen much more flagrant displays in his time. For that matter, so have I."

Maggie stood and punched his arm. It didn't hurt. She was so small compared to him, but he played along, shying away and then pouncing, wrapping her in his arms to fold her close to his heart.

"I didn't know I was getting involved with an exhibitionist." Her words were muffled against his shirt. Then she looked up at him, laughter in her eyes. "And you better not be watching any more *flagrant displays* or I'll poke your eyes out."

"Ooh. I like it when you're feisty." He kissed her, unable to stop himself.

Slade was watching their backs and there was no one better in the Pack to do so. Still, Rocky couldn't do what he wanted—which was to back her up against that tree again. So he made do with a quick kiss and a cuddle, then let her go.

"Much as I hate to, we should get back to the house. Our voyeur is waiting." Rocky held her hand and began walking out of the secluded grotto.

"I heard that." Slade's voice drifted back to them from just outside the circle of trees.

Thankfully, Maggie laughed. Rocky knew then that she'd be okay once she got used to the shifter lifestyle.

Slade took point as they began the journey back toward the house. Unlike the trip here, they didn't pause or talk much. Slade's sense of urgency communicated itself even to Maggie, and Rocky was saddened to see the lines of worry return to her lovely face. He held her hand, keeping her close to his side and kept a sharp lookout with all his senses on the surrounding woods.

He sensed the other shifters loping, flying and walking through the woods on either side of the trail. Slade had called out the cavalry to guard them as they made their way back to the house. That didn't bode well. Something was most definitely up.

It was a relief to see the house when they stepped into the small clearing in front. Slade walked them right up to the door but didn't enter. He gave Maggie a wink and a devilish smile that made her blush, and Rocky was glad his comrade had made the effort to put thoughts of danger out of her mind, if only for a moment.

Rocky shook his hand, letting Maggie be ushered away by his mother who met them at the door.

"I got a call after I met up with you at the grotto the first time. Strangers were spotted at the base of the mountain," Slade said in a hushed voice. "My men are positioned throughout the woods around your house. We'll stay on high alert until we figure out where the strangers went and if they pose any problem. I already called your dad and gave him the heads up. He and your mom are going to guard from inside the new construction. That area is vulnerable if someone is able to get too close to the house."

"Thanks, Slade." Rocky let go of the ex-soldier's hand. "Did you call the Lords?"

"Not yet. This could be nothing, but I thought it better to get your lady under cover, just in case."

"Good thinking. And thanks for the escort." They both knew Rocky was referring to the dozen or so shifters who had guarded their path from grotto to house. They'd come in force to help him protect his mate, which meant a lot to Rocky.

Slade nodded and left, slinking into the woods as only he could. Damned cat. Rocky smiled as he shook his head and went into the house.

His mom and Maggie were dealing with the cranky twins, which gave Rocky a moment to gather himself. The sight of strangers near their territory might be nothing — or it could be the showdown he'd been expecting.

Only time would tell.

CHAPTER TWELVE

Alerted by a sudden change in the energies surrounding his home, Rocky stepped out the front door a few minutes later and immediately his hackles rose. Evil was near. The *Venifucus* demon had come. Finally.

Rocky was almost glad in a way as he pulled out his cell phone and hit the speed dial that would alert Tim and Rafe. It was a pre-arranged signal he'd programmed into his phone days before. The message would be clear to them and they'd come running.

Rocky hoped his parents were okay, but he had no time to find out for sure. They'd taken up guard positions just inside the new construction, leaving Rocky and Maggie in the main part of the house with the boys. He'd thought they'd all be safe enough with Slade and his guys out there, but now Rocky wasn't so sure.

Somehow the enemy had gotten close enough for Rocky to sense them, which meant they had broken through the perimeter guards. That didn't bode well for Slade and his men.

Rocky called to Maggie, knowing the time had come to use the heartstone Tony had created for just this moment. He stepped into the doorway, facing her.

"I need your necklace, Mags. Stay here and protect the cubs. My folks won't let anyone into the house from behind, and nobody is going to get past me from here. You and the boys should be okay. Just stay in the house."

"I want to help." She squared her shoulders and he realized all over again how much he loved this fearless little human woman. He grabbed her shoulders and kissed her, fearing it might be for the last time.

But he wouldn't let it be.

"You can help best by staying with the babies. There's no stronger magic than a mother's love. You'll be able to protect them more than anyone else."

She held out the necklace that bore Tony's heartstone and he allowed her to place the pulsing red gem into his palm. A shock of power pulsed into him, up his arm and into his heart and soul. Tony's power, left for just this occasion. With the pulse of magic he felt Tony's last wishes, his love for his family — for the boys, Maggie and Rocky too — and his desire that Rocky keep them all safe. This last gift of a powerful shaman was meant to send his love over the realms separating them in one final act of protection.

The stone lost most of its unearthly glow,

remaining a beautiful gem, but much of its power was now inside Rocky. He could feel it merging and melding with his own magic, strengthening and teaching him as it found a home in his soul. This was Tony's true gift. A gift of power and the knowledge to use it. Only Tony had been strong and thoughtful enough to leave Rocky the means with which to protect the ones they both loved.

Rocky kissed her once more and turned to face the threat surrounding them now. He could feel it as his senses expanded with the rush of new magic. He could pinpoint the location of the mage and his minions. They'd come in force, but the forces of good were also on the move. Even as he recognized the various points of energy in the woods surrounding his home, some of Slade's men overcame a few of the minions, helping to better the odds. And more wolves were on the move, heading here. Tim and Rafe had mobilized their Pack.

"Face me!" Rocky shouted towards the copse of trees where he could sense the creature watching.

A few moments later, he felt the energies coalesce and move. It was his only warning as he dove away from the cabin, tearing at his clothing as he went. Shifting quickly, he spotted a tall man with potent magic that battered against his newly strengthened shields.

In weregrizzly form, he faced the demon, standing over nine feet tall on his hind legs. Even more imposing was the magic. A whole lot of very intense, protective magic. The demon wore a man's form, probably the handsome face he'd worn to bedazzle humans and shifters alike while in this realm, but as Maggie had warned, the beauty hid a soul as evil as hell itself. Rocky could sense it.

Rocky had more magical power than he'd ever had before, and it wasn't abating. The more he used, the more rose to his call. It was like nothing he'd ever experienced before. The demon backed away from him to regroup, but Rocky knew nothing would stop one sworn to the *Venifucus*. Mercy would only be turned back on the merciful. This creature had to be dealt with, lest he come back later to kill them all.

Inside the house, Maggie watched from the window, careful not to be seen. She had to protect the babies, but she also had a role to play in this if Betina was to be believed. She'd run to the phone as soon as Rocky left the house and called the older woman. Betina was already on her way.

They would form a three-pointed triangle around the battling men. Betina and Allie would each take one of the points from either side of the clearing and Maggie and the boys would complete the sacred geometric form from the house.

Maggie didn't know a great deal about magic, but she felt a buzz in the air when the triangle snapped into place. Peering out the window, she could see the two women at the edge of the woods, one on either side of the house.

A shimmer floated on the air around them and Maggie realized the same shimmer was inside the room with her and the babies. She looked at the boys, who were silent and holding hands. The shimmer was coming from *them*.

It surprised her but didn't frighten her. This was

magic, she knew. The magic her babies had been born with, thanks to their father. The shimmering light extended and grew, lancing out the sides of the house toward Allie and Betina. Walls didn't matter to the light. It connected Maggie, the babies and the women outside on some kind of spiritual plane that didn't know the meaning of walls.

She knew instinctively that the triangle contained and protected those within. It would be up to Rocky to defeat the demon but she had every faith in him.

Rocky felt the magic surround them from all sides while the demon roared in displeasure. The creature was cut off from its minions, unable to draw power from them with the death and destruction they wrought. The demon would have to face Rocky without magical support.

This made the match just about even considering the magical boost Rocky had received from Tony's heartstone. Rocky liked his chances and knew if he failed, others would pick up the fight until this demon was no more. Such was the benefit of living among the most powerful and diverse Pack on the continent. He knew the Lords would protect the twins and Maggie, or die trying.

They were on their way, but until they arrived, Rocky was the only thing standing between the demon and his new family. The love of his life and the babies he had claimed as his own. It was up to him now. He would have to either kill the bastard outright or hold off the demon until help arrived.

With that knowledge tucked close to its heart, Rocky engaged the battle. He rushed at the man, swiping through the demon's magical shields with his claws. The added magic and his own brawn mixed together to topple both the shields and the man.

Then the man morphed into the monster that lay beneath his skin and the game was on.

For long minutes, Rocky battled the horned demon whose shape was distorted and half hidden by the swirling maelstrom Maggie had described from her dreams. It was as if the demon had no true shape, but Rocky soon discovered it was able to bleed.

Blow after blow landed on its sticky, smelly hide, Rocky's claws making deadly contact. Each hit containing not only Rocky's innate brute strength, but a powerful blast of white light that parted the red and black miasma as if it was a hot knife slicing through butter. The dark cloud could not stand in the face of the shimmering light that represented Rocky's magic.

The muddy smoke began to dissipate, leaving bald patches where Rocky's claws connected solidly with the creature beneath. The demon was quickly losing its protective shield, and Rocky went in for the kill.

Blood in the air fired his grizzly instincts while the magic created vast tears in what was left of the creature's shield of protection. For that's what it was. Now ripped away by superior magic, Rocky finally understood why he couldn't see the form of the demon at first. The muddy fog was his main protection.

Without it, he could be killed in the physical plane. Rocky would leave it up to the priestesses to banish the demon's immortal soul but he would gladly take care of its earthly body.

With a new ferociousness, Rocky waged into battle, striking blow after blow for the side of light. He felt his enemy growing weaker. He knew when and how to strike the final blow and he did not hesitate. This needed to be ended here and now. Never to return.

Within one final strike, the demon's earthly body lay defeated, torn and bloody, his magic burned away by the rage of Rocky's attack. The heart stuttered and stopped as Rocky let loose a grizzly roar of triumph.

A swirling maelstrom of red and brown thundered up from the remains and dove back down at him, but Rocky's magic was strong and protected him. The magical triangle contained the fury of the demon's magic — or what was left of it that could affect the physical plane. Rocky saw Betina and Allie move in from the edge of the clearing, their hands held out as if pushing the demon's magical remains into a smaller and smaller container.

Indeed, the triangle that had surrounded them during the battle was growing smaller as the women moved forward. A sound from behind him made Rocky turn.

And there was Maggie, a baby in each arm, the third point of the triangle. Rocky stood in awe as she drew closer. The look on her face was one of utter determination. The babies in her arms were focused on the swirling, evil mist, but they weren't afraid.

Whether the magic came from the twins or from a mother's love and need to protect her babies, Rocky didn't know for sure. But it was equal to or stronger than the priestesses, fully able to keep up with the more experienced women.

The triangle became smaller and smaller until Betina stepped forward to reshape the cordon of energy. She began to sing, pure crystal notes lifting upward on the slight wind, carrying with them small pieces of the dark, evil cloud, dissipating them into another realm a bit at a time.

It took only moments, but the foreign words of the strange song, in a language Rocky could not name, removed the taint of the demon's essence completely. Rocky could sense no evil around him when Betina's song ended. The demon was gone.

Allie and Betina lowered their arms and the older woman smiled.

"That should do it. If he ever finds all the pieces of himself, he'll be limited to walking in that other realm for many centuries to come." She smiled and her eyes danced with delight. "The *Venifucus* have lost a powerful ally today."

Rocky roared in approval, still wearing his bear skin. He would change back, but first he wanted Maggie to see him—really see him—in his fur. He hadn't wanted to scare her off so he hadn't changed in front of her before now. But she would have to come to terms with the knowledge that he was a grizzly bear. And so were their sons.

Allie and Betina went to Maggie, each taking one of the babies to check them over for any signs of strain. Rocky had sniffed them already. The boys were just fine. He could feel their magical energy—so vast and powerful. They were something special, and they had connected even closer to him now that he had Tony's last gift of power within his soul.

Rocky stood calmly before Maggie, hoping she would come to him.

She didn't disappoint him. She dropped to her knees in front of him and wrapped her trembling arms around his furry neck. She gasped into his fur, emotion overcoming her now that the danger was over.

"Oh, God, Rocky. I was so scared for you," she whispered.

He moved into her embrace, trying to offer the comfort of his presence even if he couldn't hug her at the moment. That would come soon enough. First, he had to be certain the perimeter was safe. He wouldn't change back to his human form until he was sure.

Rafe and Tim came into the clearing and walked over to them. Maggie let him go and Rocky backed away

"We got the rest of his men and traced them back to their vehicles. The Pack will take care of the rest," Rafe reported.

Glad of the news, Rocky shifted back to human form. His hands were bloody, but his conscience was clear. The demon would never hurt his family—or any other shifter for that matter—ever again.

"How about Slade?" he asked, his arms around Maggie as she stood in front of him. He wasn't about to let her go anytime soon.

"He and his guys are mopping up. Nobody was seriously hurt."

"Thank the Lady for that," Rocky said, offering a silent prayer to the Mother of All who had protected the men and soldiers of the Pack.

Tim and Rafe agreed, then went to talk with their

mate, Allie. The babies were with Marissa and Joe, and the wolf Pack would handle the rest of the cleanup. Rocky was grateful. Every instinct he had called for him to be with Maggie and the cubs. He ushered her toward the house where his parents were taking the boys. He paused only a short moment retrieve his jeans and rinse his hands in the water from a garden hose. He didn't want that demon's blood inside his house.

Maggie didn't leave his side. She knew her babies were safe with their grandparents and Rocky's continued silence worried her. The whole scene she had just witnessed made her quake in her shoes if she thought about it too long. Rocky was her lifeline. Her safety in a roiling sea.

She helped him, holding the hose while he scrubbed at his hands and fingernails, getting every last bit of blood before he took the hose from her and doused his head and toso.

"Brrr. Isn't that cold?" She couldn't help but comment. It had to be near freezing out here, and yet he was nearly naked and now wet and didn't seem to mind.

"Honey, I'm a grizzly bear," he reminded her, turning off the hose and sending her an amused expression.

She remembered how he'd looked and felt in his alternate form. He'd been massive and yet, soft and furry. Almost cuddly. Not that she thought he'd enjoy that phrase. She'd keep it to herself for now. Hug the remembered feel of his soft fur to her heart.

"Is that why you call me honey?" she asked

instead, turning the subject.

He grinned and pulled her into his arms. He was still wet, but the sweater she wore protected her from the worst of it.

"It is a well known fact that bears love honey. And this bear, in particular, loves you, honey."

After the ordeal they'd been through, she could barely speak as tears welled in her eyes.

"I love you too, Rocky," she managed to choke out.

He lifted her in his arms and carried her into the house. He took her right into the bedroom and kicked the door shut with one heel while his lips sought hers.

"You're safe now, Mags," he crooned into her ear as she tried her best to climb his torso like a tree. "Nothing and no one will ever hurt you again if I have anything to say about it."

She was shaking now with reaction. "I can't believe it's finally over. All those months of running—"

"Are at an end," he confirmed, sitting down on the big bed, keeping her on his lap as he held her close. "There may be trials to come," he went on. "I won't lie to you. Being a shifter in the modern world has its dangers, and these *Venifucus* are plotting something terrible. We're fighting them. It's an ongoing thing, and our boys will be targets simply because of what they are."

"The next Lords, right?" she asked. "Because they're twins?"

"Because they're intensely magical," Rocky clarified. "And yes, because twin births are rarer than rare among shifters. They are significant because we believe they are directed by the Goddess Herself."

"They're so little. It's hard to think of them being like Tim and Rafe one day."

"But they will be. And we'll be here to guide them. To help them become the men they are destined to be." Rocky kissed to top of her head as she nestled against his chest. She felt warm and protected. Surrounded by his love.

"I like the sound of that."

CHAPTER THIRTEEN

Christmas Eve

Rocky had been working on the terabytes of information from Tony's external hard drive for some time. It would take weeks to sort through all the files and figure out what to do with the information. The Lords had tasked him with the project, since he knew Tony better than anyone.

He was working on his laptop while Maggie listened to the news from the outside world on the television in the living room. They'd been through so much in such a short amount of time. It was nice to spend a quiet moment with her in such regular, commonplace pursuits.

But then he heard something in the distance…growing nearer.

"What in the world is that?" Rocky asked, rising

from his seat on the couch. They were sitting by the fire, enjoying a few moments of privacy while his parents put the babies to bed.

"What? I don't hear anything," Maggie answered, turning off the television before joining him. He could see the concern in her eyes. She still hadn't quite recovered from the ordeal they'd been through, but she was getting a little more secure every day.

"Singing." Rocky went to the window and peered out.

A group of shifters sang carols as they hiked through the woods toward Rocky's house, giving him ample warning of their arrival. By the time they were on his doorstep, Maggie and Rocky were ready for guests. The knock on the door came as no surprise, but when Rocky opened it, the sight that greeted him did.

A large blue spruce had been transplanted from elsewhere in the forest to his front yard. On it were garlands of popcorn and berries that would no doubt feed the feather winged population the following day.

"Maggie, you've got to see this." He made room for her under his arm as she moved to his side. Her little gasp of appreciation told him she was as impressed by the gesture as he was.

Rafe and Tim stood off to one side with Allie as Betina sprouted gossamer wings that shone in the moonlight. Fluttering her wings, she lifted herself to the very tip of the tall tree and placed a magical pulse of her energy to light up the top branch like a star. Applause broke out from around the clearing and Rocky realized nearly the entire wolf Pack had come.

Allie stepped forward and held out her hands to

Maggie. "We want to welcome you and the boys to our community, Maggie. We hope you like our gift."

"We didn't think you'd mind the tree there," Rafe said as he came up behind Allie, placing one hand on her shoulder. "We can move it later if it's not exactly where you want it, but we figured this position would look nice from inside and outside."

"It looks good." Rocky leaned forward to shake Rafe's hand and then Tim's. "Thanks for doing it. I think Maggie can't be in any doubt now as to how welcome she is here." Rocky settled his arm around her shoulders.

"It's beautiful," she said with a tear in her eye and a slight hitch in her voice, clearly moved by the shifter community's gesture.

A small party followed that mostly took place outside in the snow. Maggie got into a frolicking snowball fight, though nobody was aiming to really hit anything. If Maggie was the only person bundled up tight in layer upon layer of winter clothes, nobody seemed to mind.

Marissa and Joe came outside with the babies—now wide awake and laughing at all the commotion—in their carrier, and thermal flasks full of hot mulled cider and the ingredients for s'mores. The sugary snacks were soon being toasted over an impromptu campfire in the barbeque pit at the side of the house, and Rocky knew Maggie was enjoying herself.

She settled in his embrace as they sat in front of the fire, facing the new tree somewhat distant in their front yard. Marissa and Joe kept watch over the babies, who had shifted into little bear cubs and wriggled out of their carrier. They were sniffing around the new tree and gumming some of the popcorn hanging off low branches, but Marissa's sharp eye kept them out of any real trouble.

Rocky marveled at his family—new and old—and the woman who had made this happy scene possible. Maggie was the center of his universe and he'd keep her warm and safe for as long as she'd let him. The rest of their lives... And he prayed they would live a long, long time.

"Rocky," she whispered, clutching his arm. "Do you see him?"

He followed her line of sight to the new tree with its magically glowing star on top and his heart nearly stopped. "I do, honey," he whispered.

There was no need to say more. They both saw the ghostly outline of Tony, bending to touch each of his sons, as if giving them a benediction from beyond. Marissa and Joe didn't seem to see anything amiss, but it looked like the babies were very aware of their ghostly visitor as they moved into Tony's phantom touch, trying to lick his hands with their tiny grizzly bear tongues.

He spent a long time admiring his boys before standing once again and facing the fire. Rocky was frozen in place, afraid if he moved he'd shatter the moment.

He could see through his old friend, and the magic of the glowing star atop the tree seemed to illuminate Tony's outline as he smiled and nodded in Rocky and Maggie's direction. Did he approve of their new relationship? Rocky wasn't sure.

Then Tony took all doubt away, sending them

both two thumbs up—a gesture he'd often used to convey happiness and approval while they were growing up. That gesture and the broad smile on his face left Rocky in no doubt. This was Tony and he was giving them his blessing.

"Thanks, brother," Rocky whispered, tightening his arms around Maggie as she began to weep. "We really miss you."

Tony acknowledged his words with a smiling nod as he faded from view.

Maggie turned in Rocky's arms and buried her face against his chest, crying, when he noticed a gentle presence come up beside them and sit.

"Don't worry, Margaret," Betina said softly. "Your first love sees what happens here and approves. You will see him again, both here and in the next world."

The words and Betina's comforting, magical presence made Maggie stop crying, thank goodness. She wiped her eyes as she sat up again and faced the older woman who had revealed beyond a shadow of doubt tonight that she was fey. Rocky didn't quite know what to make of her now. Fey were among the most magical of creatures, rarely seen and seldom involved in earthly affairs. That she was here now, with the Lords in this time of increased danger, seemed ominous. And yet hopeful at the same time.

When she saw she had Maggie's attention, Betina went on. "I've heard Antonio was a gifted shaman. I have seen the truth of it myself here tonight. He left a part of his soul in this realm, probably to look after his boys. He will watch them from afar as they grow, and occasionally—at very special times—he may be able to communicate with them. This is something only the most powerful of magics can accomplish, which should give all *were* hope for the future. Twins born of such a sire will be strong leaders for the new generation."

"But I'm with Rocky now. I love Tony. But I love Rocky too. I love them both. I think I always have." Maggie's voice shook with emotion and Betina reached out to touch her shoulder.

This was the sticking point. Rocky knew Maggie would never really be his until she'd come to terms with the conflict within her heart.

"He knows, dear. He's always known that you love Rocky as much as you love him." Betina smiled and it felt like the whole world was filled with a magical sparkle, even in the pale moonlight of a cold winter's night. "The heart knows no limits when love is true."

Betina got up and walked away, her words ringing in their ears.

Rocky held Maggie as a light dusting of snow began to fall.

"I loved Tony and that will never change," Maggie said after long moments.

"I know," Rocky replied solemnly. "I don't want that to change. I loved him too. He will always be my brother. But there's room in our hearts for more, honey, just like Betina said."

Maggie turned and kissed him, and he had his answer. Her mind was settled and her heart open wide. Rocky could feel the last little barrier between them fall and his heart filled with joy at the love they both felt.

Wrapped up in each other, only Betina saw the tall, glowing shadow of a man smiling down on them from just out of reach.

# # #

ABOUT THE AUTHOR

Bianca D'Arc has run a laboratory, climbed the corporate ladder in the shark-infested streets of Manhattan, studied and taught martial arts, and earned the right to put a whole bunch of letters after her name, but she's always enjoyed writing more than any of her other pursuits.

She grew up and still lives on Long Island, where she keeps busy with an extensive garden, several aquariums full of very demanding fish, and writing her favorite genres of paranormal, fantasy and sci-fi romance.

Bianca loves to hear from readers and can be reached through Facebook, her Yahoo group or through the various links on her website.

Visit her website at:

WWW.BIANCADARC.COM

OTHER TITLES BY BIANCA D'ARC

Tales of the Were
Lords of the Were
Inferno
The Purrfect Stranger
Rocky

Brotherhood of Blood
One & Only
Rare Vintage
Phantom Desires
Sweeter Than Wine
Forever Valentine
Wolf Hills

Dragon Knights
Maiden Flight
Border Lair
The Ice Dragon
Prince of Spies
Wings of Change
FireDrake
Dragon Storm
Keeper of the Flame

Jit'Suku Chronicles: Arcana
End of the Line
King of Swords
King of Cups
King of Clubs

Coming Soon:

Tales of the Were
Slade
Available in ebook – March 2013
In Print April 2013

Dragon Knights
The Dragon Healer
Available in ebook – July 2013
In print September 2013

Dragon Knights
Master at Arms
Available in ebook – August 2013
In print September 2013

Jit'Suku Chronicles: Arcana
King of Stars
Available in ebook – Summer 2013

Brotherhood of Blood:
Wolf Quest
Available in ebook – December 2013
In Print October 2014

We hope you'll enjoy this excerpt from a short story set in the world of Bianca D'Arc's *Jit'Suku Chronicles*...

End of the Line
by
Bianca D'Arc

Chapter One

She saw the incoming fire too late to save her ship. The one-man fighter was going down, and if she didn't pop her canopy in the next five milliseconds, she was going with it.

Lisbet realized she had no choice. Hitting the CATASTROPHIC FAILURE button, she checked herself out of her ride split seconds before it blew into a million little weightless bits. Out in the nothingness of space near the galactic Rim, she was in no man's land where rescue was hard to come by. She had either a long wait or a slow death to look forward to in the next few hours.

The enemy jits had won this battle, though hopefully not the war. Skirmishes on the Rim had escalated in recent years as the jit'suku empire looked for ways to gain a foothold in the Milky Way galaxy. The expansion from their home galaxy was fueled by the comparative ease of travel via an inconvenient wormhole and several jumpoints that had been created before humans had realized how the jit'suku truly viewed the human race.

Inferior. That's what the jits thought of humans. Inferior in every way to their war-mongering race. Though they looked very human in appearance – if built on a bit larger scale than most humans – jit'suku society was one that most humans had a hard time understanding. They prized warriors and seemed to scoff at diplomats or anyone who wanted to negotiate peaceful coexistence. The only thing the jits understood was conquest, it seemed.

Which was why they'd been fighting so long and so hard out here, on the Rim of the Milky Way galaxy. Lisbet was just the latest in a nearly endless rotation of human fighter pilots who had drawn the dreaded, but vital, duty of patrolling the Rim.

Vast reaches of emptiness between nearly lawless stations, dangerous jumpoints, and the occasional star system, Rim duty was enough to drive anyone crazy. But she welcomed the emptiness of space and the loneliness of her own thoughts after this humiliation.

She'd been on this patrol for over a week with nothing to report. Then this.

A jit'suku battle cruiser had appeared as if from out of nowhere, and blasted her before she could even get a message out. He'd been lying in wait behind an asteroid. Lisbet had known to be cautious, but honestly, her thoughts had been elsewhere. As soon as she spotted the giant ship lumbering out from behind cover of the asteroid, it had already been too late. Her signals bounced back – jammed. A moment later, a blanket of weapons fire appeared on her screens – sent the distance between the two ships in all her possible trajectories. She was blown already, and she knew it.

Popping her canopy and stranding herself in the middle of nowhere in the emergency pod had been her only choice. Not a great one, but there'd been no other way to get clear of all the incoming fire. The bastard giving orders on that battle cruiser hadn't been taking any chances that she'd get clear and report back. He'd thrown everything but the kitchen sink at her and she hadn't stood a chance.

"Human, this is Captain Fedroval of the battle cruiser *Fedroval's Legacy*. Warrior to warrior, I give you the choice. Would you prefer the fast death of missile fire or the slow death of suffocation when your air runs out?"

For a moment, Lisbet thought of ignoring the short-range communication from the cruiser. He was still blocking her long-range transmitter, but he'd allowed her enough bandwidth to broadcast to his ship. Big of him. Damned jit'suku bastard.

"How do you know I'm not the advance scout of a much larger force? Could be my battalion is on my heels and will pick me up after they blow you to kingdom come." Oh, how she wished that were true. She'd get a lot of satisfaction right now at seeing the jit'suku ship blown into a million pieces.

There was a slight delay in the answer she'd expected would come back right away. He probably knew she was bluffing. If he'd been hiding out behind that asteroid for any length of time, he had to know hers was merely a patrol craft on a regular route.

"Who is this? What is your name, rank and gender?"

He sounded mad now, for some reason she

couldn't imagine. And why would he ask her gender? That seemed odd in the extreme. But she'd play along. She'd be alone out here for a long while – if he let her live after this encounter – and she was going to have a lot of time, alone with her thoughts, before her air ran out. Might as well talk to someone while she had company, even if he was a damned jit.

"Lieutenant Lisbet Duncan of Earth. And I'm female, not that it should matter to you. I'm a qualified pilot who graduated top of my class from pilot training."

While there had always been a lot more males drawn to military life than females, Lisbet wasn't too much of an oddity. Many women had the natural skills needed to fly shuttles and other spacecraft. She was unique in that she'd requested fighter duty. She liked shooting at things and would've tried for a gunner position on one of the big battleships if she hadn't qualified as a pilot.

"Prepare for retrieval." The order was brusque and his harsh voice sounded even angrier.

"Now just wait a damn minute!"

A moment later she saw two small craft launch from the battleship and head straight for her. The bastards were going to pick up her pod. She was going to be a prisoner of war.

Dammit!

Although... it was probably better than dying alone in the vastness of space. At least if they picked her up, she might have a chance to do some damage to them before she died. She didn't like the idea of being tortured, but she'd trained for it, like all the other pilots, and thought she was mostly prepared.

She didn't know much anyway. She wasn't privy to any battle strategies or troop deployment information. She only knew her current mission and those she'd been on previously. Not much of value to the jit'suku empire.

Sure enough, the two craft flanked her and deployed sturdy microfilament netting that encompassed her pod. As soon as she was secure, they flew her back toward the cruiser. The ship was even larger than she'd thought. It had the latest in jit technology, from what she could see of its outboard arrays. This was no battered old warhorse. This ship was battle ready and gleaming, though she could see a few spots where repairs had been made after engagements with human forces, no doubt.

The two patrol craft deposited her inside a gleaming hangar bay, bumping her only once as they set her down. The nets retracted and they parked on either side of her ship. She waited patiently inside her pod, gathering what little information she could. Her instruments told her the hangar bay was pressurized with a breathable atmosphere, and she saw big jit'suku men working on various craft parked nearby without breathing gear.

The hangar bay had a giant force field at one end, keeping the air in. Nice. On human battleships, the hangar bays were kept at zero atmosphere. Pilots loaded into the canopies above and were dropped down and secured to the fuselages below via a small chamber that was sealed and then evacuated of its precious air before opening to the hangar deck below.

The pilots who had caught her pod climbed out of their cockpits and moved closer to investigate. One made a sign for her to pop her lid and she shook her head, refusing. They went on like this for a few minutes, arguing via sign language through the window until suddenly everyone on the flight deck jumped to attention.

At the far end of the long deck, Lisbet could see a giant of a man – even among the very large jit'suku warriors – coming toward her at a fast pace. He looked absolutely furious. And handsome.

Damn. Why did she have to notice how handsome he was? She should be completely immune to men after what she'd been through. But this guy – this angry guy – flipped her switches in all the right ways.

He grabbed a piece of equipment as he went, nearly tearing it out of a tech's hands. It had to be magnetic because it clamped onto her canopy the moment he touched the device to her hull. He held something on a wire up to his mouth and suddenly his voice boomed through her internal speakers.

"Stop playing games and come out of there now or I'll have you cut out."

Lisbet sighed. She'd have to open the hatch sooner or later. She admitted, if only to herself, that she was scared. These jit'suku were all massive and everyone she could see so far was male. She had no idea what they had in mind for her, but she wasn't looking forward to finding out. Still, she couldn't hide in here forever. The time had come to take her punishment. Whatever that might entail.

Releasing the hatch, the canopy popped with a hiss of equalizing air. Whirring gears indicated the hatch was rolling up and back the way it had been designed to do. As it cleared, she got her first really good look at the glowering man with the captain's insignia on his uniform.

Oh, boy. The captain himself had come down to get her. No wonder the crew had all jumped at his entrance. Lisbet wondered what she'd done to rate the captain's attention.

Pushing herself out of the seat, she stood within the canopy. She should have been taller than anyone on the deck from where she was, but she hadn't counted on these giant jit'suku.

The captain's eyes met hers and time stood still for a breathless moment.

His eyes were dark. The dark of space with a hint of golden brown that made them somehow warm. His molten gaze would have been inviting in another setting. As it was, she could see the flare of gold in his gaze as his expression tightened.

He held out one impatient hand and she took it before she could think better of it. He assisted her in the big step over the canopy lip and down onto the deck of the cruiser. She was truly in enemy territory now. Goddess help her.

Enjoy this excerpt from Bianca D'Arc's first book set in the critically acclaimed, EPPIE and CAPA award winning *Dragon Knights* series...

Maiden Flight
by
Bianca D'Arc
Copyright 2006 Bianca D'Arc. All Rights Reserved.

Chatper One

Belora tracked the stag through the forest. Carefully chosen for this hunt, the stag was older, past the prime of his life, and would feed her small family of two for more than a month if she and her mother used it wisely. On silent feet, she followed him down to the water, a small trickle of stream that fed into the huge lake beyond.

Taking careful aim with her bow, Belora offered up a silent prayer of hope and thanks to the Mother of All and to the spirit of the stag that would give its life so that she and her mother could live. She loosed the arrow, watching it sail home to her target, embedding itself deep in the stag's heart. Her aim was true.

As expected, the stag ran off, pumping away the last of its life in a desperate attempt to escape. She followed, saddened by the poor creature's flight but knowing it must be so. The old stag ran into a clearing, flailing wildly. He was nearing his end, she knew, and again she prayed to the Mother of All that it would be swift.

The stag faltered in its running stride, a shadow seeming to pass over from above. A moment later, the stag was gone, clasped tightly in the talons of a magnificent dragon winging away toward the far end of the small clearing.

Belora took off as fast as her tired feet would carry her, following the dragon who had stolen her prize.

Coming out of his swooping dive, the dragon pinned the stag's quivering body between the long talons of his right foreleg. He'd made a clean kill, stabbing the beast through the heart with his sharp-edged digit even before lifting it into the air. It struggled for a few moments more, then lay dead in his grasp. The dragon rejoiced in the skillful kill, chortling smoke into the air above him.

He came to a neat landing at the far end of the small clearing and dropped the dead stag to the ground with satisfaction. That was when he noticed the little stick protruding from the other side of the beast. It was an arrow. Drat.

"Oh no, you don't!"

The irate, high pitched human voice made the dragon shift his gaze upward to look quizzically at the small female now facing him with her hands perched in tight fists on her hips. A longbow was slung over her shoulder.

"I shot that stag well before you swooped down and picked him up. He's my kill. What's more, he will feed me and my mother for a month or more. For you, he's just a snack! You leave him be. He's mine."

She shook with indignant anger and it was truly a

sight to behold. Luminous green eyes sparkled in her pretty, flushed face. She seemed to have no fear of him, mighty dragon that he was, with blood on his talons and fire in his belly. She clearly had courage, and it impressed him. Few humans, much less small females, dared to deal with dragons directly.

He could feel her anger, and a rudimentary channel of thought opened between her mind and his. She was one of the rare humans then, who could communicate with his kind. This intrigued him even more, and one thought kept running through his mind — Gareth had to see this.

"What's your name, pretty one?" The dragon spoke directly into Belora's mind, surprising her a bit, but her mother had told her stories about the dragon she'd known as a child. Belora knew dragons communicated with humans mind to mind. It was part of their ancient magic.

"I'm Belora." She renewed her forceful stance. She could not let this dragon sense any fear. She needed that stag. "Will you yield the stag to me?"

"Why are you not afraid of my kind? Do you know dragons?"

That wasn't an answer, but she supposed she should at least be polite. Her mother had taught her the etiquette required when dealing with dragons.

"Not I, sir. My mother knew a dragon once though. She told me about your kind." Belora knew she had to convince him soon. The longer this dragged on, the more likely he was to haul her before some tribunal for poaching. "So what about the stag?"

"From where I stand, it was my talon that made

the kill. Not your puny arrow. *But you have a good argument. I'll give you that."*

The dragon moved closer to her as she fumed in response, but she didn't realize she was being set up until it was much too late. While she argued with him, the dragon moved closer still, until he had the stag wrapped in the talons on one huge foreleg and she was much too close to the other. As she realized her mistake, he swooped in and made his move.

He reached out quicker than thought and snapped the padded digits of his left foreleg around her waist, trapping her arms inside the cage his wickedly sharp talons made around her. She screamed in frustration and more than a bit of fear. The dragon only chuckled.

"Don't worry, little one." His voice was gentle in her mind, as if trying to calm her.

The dragon beat his huge wings two or three times and then they were airborne. She couldn't help the little yelp of fright that escaped as her feet left the ground. He could easily open his claw and drop her to the ground far below. That would solve his problem quite easily, she thought with growing horror.

But dragons were supposed to be noble creatures! In all the tales she'd heard about them, she'd never heard of one going to such lengths to toy with a human before. They were mankind's friends, not enemies, and they weren't supposed to go around snatching up maidens only to hurtle them to their deaths.

As they gained altitude and he did not release her to die a nasty and painful death, she began to calm.

She was held in one front claw, the slain deer in the other. She looked around and realized she had never seen such a beautiful sight. The view from above was breathtaking. She could see the huge mountain lake as they approached it, and if she craned her neck to look behind, she could see the forest canopy, green and fertile, hiding the secrets of the creatures that lived within.

She and her mother lived there, under the thick cover of trees, and had for many years. It was their haven, their home. Nothing as magical as this had ever happened to Belora, living isolated in the forest, and she decided to enjoy this moment out of time, flying high above the world. She would likely never have the chance again, for it was rare that a dragon transported a human that was not their knight partner. She knew that from the stories and legends the old ones told of knights and dragons. Even her mother—who had been friends with a dragon in her youth—had never flown with one. It was a rare and magical experience.

"Do you like the view, little one?"

"It's beautiful!" Belora had to shout to be heard over the racing wind.

The dragon chuckled, thoughtfully directing the stream of smoke out behind him and away from her. She realized from the gesture that he was well used to being around humans and carrying them as he flew, but she guessed he didn't carry too many in his claws. The legends all said knights rode on the backs of their dragon partners.

"Where are you taking me?" She pulled her attention from the gorgeous vista long enough to question her predicament. If he was taking her to a tribunal, she was in big trouble. She'd rather know now if she would be facing arrest when they landed.

"Fear not, little one. I said you had a good case for the stag. *We will let the knight decide.*"

They cruised over the edge of the large mountain lake. The water sparkled below as the dragon dropped lower. A moist breeze off the water teased her senses.

"What knight?" That didn't sound good.

Rather than calming her fears, the news that there was a knight in the area only made things worse. She'd been poaching, plain and simple. Mere peasants weren't allowed to kill the deer to feed their families, but the dragons were welcome to them as a snack at any time.

"That knight," the dragon thought back at her. It took her a moment to understand his meaning, but when she looked down and just ahead of their path, she saw a sleek male body cutting through the waters of the lake. He swam like a fish or like one of the great sea creatures she had heard stories about. She found herself distracted by the sun gleaming off the powerful muscles of his arms as he sliced through the water, heading for shore. Something about the man's hard body pulled at her most feminine core, though she was inexperienced with men, in general.

"I am Kelvan and that's Gareth, my knight."

19021678R00097

Made in the USA
Charleston, SC
03 May 2013